KNUCKLEHEAD NOIR

COFFIN HOP PRESS

Also available from

COFFIN HOP PRESS

NEW CRIME. NEW WEIRD. NEW PULP.

Death By Drive-In: 22 B-Movie Inspired Tales of Terror

Tall Tales of the Weird West

AB Negative: An Anthology of Alberta Crime

Fishing With the Devil by Robert Bose

Con Morte by Axel Howerton

Rocket Ryder & Little Putt-Putt Go Down Swinging by Timothy Friend

It's A Weird Winter Wonderland

Infractus by Sarah L. Johnson

Kill As You Go by Therese Greenwood

The Dame Was Trouble: Canada's Best Female Crime Writers

Baby, It's Cold Outside: Dark Tales of Christmas Crime

Futility: Orange Planet Horror

Sleeping Underwater by Ryan States

KNUCKLEHEAD NOIR

COFFIN HOP PRESS

Calgary, Alberta
CANADA

Coffin Hop Press
200 Rivervalley Crescent SE
Calgary, Alberta CANADA T2C 3K8
www.coffinhop.com
mailto:info@coffinhop.com

A Proudly Canadian Publisher
Cover Design ©2019 Coffin Hop Press
Cover Art: ©2019 Tom Bagley

Interior Elements: Shutterstock ID: 1464588611; 495201538; 243736603

Book Layout ©2019 Coffin Hop Press

Knucklehead Noir / Various —1st ed. Paperback
ISBN: 978-1-988987-19-4

Strictly for the hell of it.

Her mouth tasted like doublemint gum masking tobacco, one of Charlie's favorite combinations.

— Scott Phillips "The Ice Harvest"

Table of Contents

FOREWORD

As a kid in the 1970s, I got it into my head that the coolest damn thing I could possibly do would be to ride my bike (with banana seat and sissy bar, of course) off the roof of our house like Evel Knievel. It went about as well as his jump over the fountains at Caesar's Palace, although significantly less spectacular. I could barely walk for about four days afterwards.

So yeah, I've always had a soft spot for dumb people doing dumb things – and I especially enjoy dumb people doing dumb *criminal* things.

I can claim two dumb crimes of my own, by the way.

The first was entirely accidental (I swear!), while the second was driven by my youthful desire to both be cool and see naked ladies.

My first dumb crime involved strolling around the five-and-dime and looking at all the cool stuff I couldn't afford. I was probably eight years old and had wandered away from my dad. It was winter, so I was sporting my heavy coat. Intrigued by a display of incredibly tiny padlocks in blister packs hanging on the rack, I plucked a package down to get a closer look. The lock suddenly slid out of its packaging and fell right down the sleeve of my coat. I went into a panic, glancing furtively around the store. I figured if I fished the lock out of my sleeve and tried to stuff it back into the package, I'd get pinched for trying to steal it. Instead, I hung the now-empty package back on its hook, then, keeping my arm in an awkward raised position to prevent the lock from sliding out of my sleeve, found my dad and nervously walked around with him until he wrapped up his shopping and we left. I felt guilty about sort-of stealing that lock for months afterward.

The second time around, I had just started at a new school. I was nine years old and desperately wanted to make friends. A cool kid in my class stopped me after school and asked if I wanted to go with him to the drugstore down the street. I knew full well that the place had a swell spinner rack full of comics, and hey, *a cool kid wants me to go with him!* How could I refuse? We walked to the store and once inside, Mr. Coolio immediately scoped out the location of the two employees, then told me

I had to create a distraction while he stole the new Playboy calendar. I hesitated, of course, but my burgeoning interest in the female of the species combined with my hopes of being on Team Cool Kid and thereby not getting my ass kicked repeatedly throughout the school year won out. While the cool kid headed for the magazine rack, I knocked over a display of candy, very effectively providing cover for the theft. I gave the cool kid a head start outta there, then left the store myself. We ducked into a nearby alley to check out the naked delights, but I just felt awful. I was a regular customer at the store and felt like I'd never be able to set foot in the joint again, and that meant having to go elsewhere to buy the latest issues of *Sad Sack* or *Spooky, the Tuff Little Ghost*. My life had been wrecked by my criminal behavior.

Shit – what's the statute of limitations on this stuff? Forget I said anything and go read some *Knucklehead Noir*.

Scott S. Phillips, January 2019

Two Kangaroos Chained to a Piss Pot

Jason Pearce

"Ho ho ho. Here comes Santy Clause."

Holy shit on a stick, it's Ang. Eighteen months early, if I'm counting right, wearing the same clothes he was that day the Mounties dragged him off. The only new thing is the vinyl bag with the stencilled lettering. *Newfoundland and Labrador Department of Corrections*. It's got to be some kind of collector's item.

"Ang! What are you doing here?"

"They take pity on people this time of year. Good will to men and all that."

"It's a Christmas miracle!" Mudder says, eyes all watery. She rushes forward and buries her face in Ang's chest. Ang returns the hug, though he doesn't look entirely comfortable with it after all this time away.

"Take it easy, Mudder. I'm not in the door yet."

Best of all, Ang brought presents. I don't know how he managed it, but that's what's in the bag. When Mudder suggests we wait until Christmas morning, Ang won't hear of it.

"Fuck tradition. It's not every day a man is reunioned with his family."

"It *is* nice to have everybody together," Mudder says.

"Four out of five ain't bad," Ang says.

Mudder's face drops the way it does when anybody acknowledges the existence of the Old Man.

"No," she says. "This is all of us. We can open the gifts now."

Wish is the most excited. He's only ten. He bounces on the kitchen chair as Ang lays a tiny, newspaper-wrapped bundle in front of him. Paper flies, revealing an otherwise normal toothbrush with the handle sharpened to a dagger point.

Mudder pokes Wish in the ribs. "Manners, Aloysius. What do you say?"

"Thanks," Wish says. "What is it?"

"That there's a shank," Ang says. He grabs the brush end of the shank, thrusts the dagger point into thin air and gives it a twist. "Some guy messes with you, stick this between his ribs. He won't mess with you again, I guarantee you."

He grabs an empty teacup from the table and drops the shank into it, brush end up. "Best of all, it's perfectly discreet. You store it like that, nobody will give it a second look."

"I love it!" Wish crows, eyes alight.

"Oh, Angus," Mudder says. "Very thoughtful."

"You next."

Mudder's is a pair of blaze orange slippers, a bit like those Crocs you see people wearing, only without the holes that make them look like spaghetti strainers.

"100% silicon," Ang says. "Guaranteed to never mildew or rot."

Standard issue from Her Majesty's Penitentiary, from what I've heard. The top of the slippers used to say the full name of the place, but Ang has filed off the second half of the letters until they just say *Her Majesty*. Mudder runs her fingers over the raised lettering like somebody reading *Letters to Penthouse* in Braille.

"They're lovely. Makes me feel like royalty!"

Mine is a little easier to predict. As soon as Ang lays the roughly wrapped package in my hand, I can tell from the size and weight that it's smokes. A full pack. It would have taken him more than a few canteen credits to buy those.

"For us to share later," Ang says. "You and me, we got some business to discuss."

"It's the cybercrime you got to stay clear of. All that stuff is tracked."

"Like the ATMs." Right away, I regret saying anything.

"Don't get me started on the ATMs," Ang says. "How was I to know they mark your envelope?"

It's true. That high-pitched machine gun sound you hear after you push the envelope into the deposit slot? That could be anything. How was Ang to know it was a computer typewriter engraving the empty envelope with his account number? Everything would have worked just fine if not for that one little thing.

"Yep," I say. "That was some plan."

"It was brilliant! Think about it. You key in five hundred bucks as the amount, deposit the empty envelop and withdraw five hundred bucks cash. Three times, Hammy. Three times I done it before the tellers started the Monday morning shift and checked the weekend deposits. Fifteen hundred big ones. I should have left for Mexico when I had the chance."

Math was never my strong suit. I take Ang's word for it when it comes to numbers.

"The parole officer wanted to know if I learned my lesson. Yessir, I most certainly did. Only it's not the lesson he thinks. You know what I learned, Hammy?"

"Stay away from cybercrime."

"Thank you," Ang says. "Cash and low-end consumer goods is the way to go. Ain't nobody tracking those."

"Don't cash have serial numbers?" I ask.

"Sure, but who tracks them? It's not like you drop a ten spot for a pack of smokes and they scribble down the serial numbers before they put it in the till."

"Holy shit," I say. "You're right."

Ang takes a deep draw on his smoke, the red ember burning to the edge of the butt. He grabs another from the pack on the porch railing and lights it off the first one.

"That's not the best part, Hammy. This being Christmas Eve, the credit union's not open tomorrow. And thanks to me, ain't nobody trusting the ATM these days. So, unless Eldon is dumb enough to take the cash receipts home, that till of his should be fatter than a Christmas turkey."

My jaw hangs slacker than a pimp's conscience as I marvel at Ang's smarts. You can never keep a man like Ang down. All that time sitting in Her Majesty's, he could have been moaning and crying about how unfair the system is. Not my brother. He puts his two and a half years to good use, learning what he can and planning for a better life on the outside. Inspirational, really.

"Are you saying what I think you're saying?" I ask.

Ang leans on the porch rail and blows three perfect smoke rings. I can't help reaching out and running my finger through one of them.

"Let me put it this way. If you want a real Christmas miracle, you got to get off your arse and do it yourself."

We wait until Mudder and Wish are both asleep, of course. We also know better than to walk out the main road. Even after midnight, there's still people coming and going from relatives' houses. Last thing we need is somebody saying, "Oh yes, we saw the Pottle brothers strolling down the road with two burlap sacks and a set of bolt cutters."

We take the old wood truck route even though it's twice as long. All you ever see on that is the odd Skidoo or ATV, which you can hear coming a mile away. The skidoo treads tamp down the snow nicely, and we only have to dive into the brush twice to avoid being seen by whoever is zooming past. We make excellent time. The moon is still high when we reach the highway, no more than a couple hundred feet away from Eldon's Gas and Convenience. Once we're certain there are no cars coming, we scoot down the roadside to Eldon's backdoor.

It's so smart of Ang to think of the bolt cutters. They've been in the shed since the Old Man's days at the Mill, which is literally longer ago than I can remember. I'd pretty much forgot they were there, but Ang knew right where to look. They work even better than he said they would. Eldon's industrial grade lock drops to the ground.

"I guess the miserable old prick was good for something," I say.

Ang stops halfway through the doorway and turns back to look at me. I can see the whites of his eyes despite the near perfect darkness.

"Who? What are you talking about?"

"The Old Man. He stole them cutters from the Mill, didn't he?"

"That's our father," Ang says. "Show some respect."

"He could be dead for all I care. What'd he ever do for us?"

Ang brandishes the bolt cutters. "He left us these, didn't he?"

"Alright," I say. "Thank you Fodder, wherever you is, for the gift of these wonderful bolt cutters."

"That's better," Ang says. "Now, come on. The night's not getting any younger."

We can't risk flashlights, so we have to operate by guesswork in the dark. I stuff my mitts into my coat pocket and feel my way around, grasping at a bunch of wooden poles that could only be mop and broom handles. Ang is two steps ahead of me, pushing aside the folding door that opens to the store's one checkout. There's just enough light coming in through the front window for us to make out the shape of the cash register on the countertop. Ang turns his head my way. It's too dark to see his face, but I can tell from the way he clucks his tongue that he's giving me that famous wink of his.

"Watch a pro in action," he says.

My brother is a shadowy work of art as he raises his hand into the air and brings his forefinger straight down onto a random cash register button. Other than the click of the plastic button, nothing happens. Ang hits another button, only this time without the dramatic flair. Still nothing. He tries a dozen more plastic clicks before bringing his clenched fist down hard onto the keypad. He's rewarded with a loud pop. I'm hopeful for a minute, but then I realize it's just one of Ang's knuckles cracking.

"Fuck me," he says. "It looks so easy on TV."

"There's a keyhole on the front of the drawer," I say. "I seen it the other day."

"Not bad," Ang says. "You might have a career in this yet."

"Thanks. Should we pick the lock?"

"Not in the dark. Watch this."

Ang slides his hands under opposite sides of the black mass which is the cash register. He grunts and strains, his teeth catching the light. The register does not move. It must be bolted to the counter.

I nudge Ang with the bolt cutters. "We could cut it off."

"I got a better idea. Give me those and stand back."

He hefts the cutters overhead and brings them down like a circus strongman wielding a giant sledgehammer. The cutters bounce but do the job. The cash register jangles with breaking plastic and metal. Ang tosses the bolt cutters aside and pulls on the drawer.

"Blood of a bitch! It's empty."

The bottom drops out of my stomach. "Eldon took the till home."

"Probably sleeps with the money under his pillow. In case he wakes up in the mood to fuck it."

"Maybe there's a safe here somewhere."

"Not likely," Ang says. "The safe would be at his house."

"It's a frigging convenience store," I say. "There must be something worth stealing here."

Ang hoots and slaps me on the back. "Hell, yeah! Beer and smokes."

The shelf with all the smokes is right behind us, protected by nothing more than a plastic panel that Ang pulls off on his first try. There are at least forty packs. They all go into my burlap sack. I hope there aren't too many packs of those god-awful menthol things.

"To the beer cooler," Ang announces, like some big shot general leading his troops to battle.

The beer cooler has a padlock on it, but the bolt cutters dispatch that right away. There are only six cases left, which makes sense on Christmas Eve, but it's plenty. We're only two men, and there are limits to what we can carry up the old woods road.

"Take a deep breath," Ang says as we head out the back door. "This is going to be one bitch of a workout."

Ang wasn't kidding about the workout. After lugging three cases of beer and a burlap sack of smokes up a snowy road, my arms are starting to cramp. When I finally drop my cargo behind our shed, my arms hang off my sides like dead snakes.

"Now what?" I ask.

"What do you think? Get this stuff inside and have a look."

There's no way we can take it in the house. Mudder would freak out for sure. It's the shed for us. The one place she never goes to. It has no windows and is so far back from the road it might as well be a soundproof bunker.

Ang opens the door and steps inside. I hand him the beer cases one by one. Only once all the beer is loaded in do we close the door, eager to see what beer brand we've ended up with. Ang yanks the pull chain for the lights. After the better part of three hours in the dark, the blue and gold labelling on the beer cases is almost too much for my eyes.

"What the everlasting fuck is Foster's?" Ang asks.

"What? No."

It is Foster's. I should have expected as much. Eldon always runs out of the good brands on Christmas Eve, leaving the stuff nobody ever buys. Why he bothers stocking Foster's in the first place is a mystery.

"It's from Australia," I say. "The boys say it's made from kangaroo piss."

Ang tears the flap off the topmost case and fishes out a bottle of Foster's. He throws his head back and hoists the bottle, draining it in one go. The belch that follows is like a release valve after all that time in Her Majesty's.

"Hammy, my boy, if kangaroo piss tastes like this, I say we go to Austria and capture a couple. We'll keep them chained to a piss pot out back. Now pass me another, if you would be so kind."

We've drunk ourselves sober. I've heard about this. Your liver or pancreas or whatever gets used to the beer, so you kind of level off for a while. We probably turned that corner well after sun-up, not that either of us would know where the sun is right now. We have all we need in the shed. Back when he was still around, this was where the Old Man went to get clear of us. He spared no expense. There's electrical for the lights and radio, a pot belly stove that burns wood for heat and a party-sized Coleman cooler that we fill to the brim with beer and snow. There's even a urinal in the back corner, hooked directly to the family septic tank. We could ride out doomsday in here as long as neither of us needs to take a dump.

I've lost track of time when a knock comes on the door. A vague sense of panic tugs at the edges of my mind. Neither of us is up to any sudden movements. Ang shuffles to the door and opens it a crack. Daylight and our little brother's voice invade the shed.

"Mudder wants to know what you're doing in there."

"Nothing," I say. "Go back in the house."

"Mudder said we can't eat Christmas dinner until you come in."

"Alright," Ang says. "Give us a minute."

Wish looks back as I'm closing the door. "Youse got beer in there. I seen it."

"You never seen nothing."

"Mudder's not going to like it."

"Mudder don't have to know," Ang says. "Got that?"

"Can I have the empties when you're done?"

Ang winks and gives the OK sign. “Sure, kid. Just keep this on the down low, alright?”

The air in the house is heavy with steam. It condenses on the windows and trickles down in tiny rivers. Salt beef and root vegetable smells waft from the stove, blending with the fatty crisp scent of the chicken or turkey roasting in the oven. Mudder’s been cooking her heart out. “Where you been?” she asks me.

“Out to the shed.”

“You were gone before I got up.”

“It’s a really nice shed.”

This explanation must be good enough because Mudder just grunts and gestures for us to sit down. She lays a heaping plate of food in front of Angus, and he digs right in. She’s laying a second plate in front of me when she steps back and tilts her head to one side. She caught the scent of the beer. It’s too late to start breathing through my nose.

“Oh, Ambrose. You said you wouldn’t.”

“Wouldn’t what?”

“You went and done it anyway.”

“Done what?”

“You made another bucket of homebrew. And on the Lord’s birthday!”

Ang puts down his fork and finishes chewing the hunk of salt beef in his mouth. He reaches for a napkin and, realizing there isn't one, dabs at his mouth with the edge of the tablecloth. When he speaks, his words are perfectly clear.

"Actually, Mudder, it was my fault. Young Hammy here was saving it for New Year's. It were me that begged him to crack the seal on Christmas. After all that time in Her Majesty's, I could use a bit of refreshment."

Classic Ang. Enough beer to knock out a moose, yet he gets all calm and sophisticated. James Bond in a Blue Oyster Cult t-shirt.

Mudder's not having it. She shakes her head. "Sweat off the devil's brow, that stuff."

"Compared to prison hooch," Ang says, "it's as sweet as the tears of Saint Anne."

"God save you," Mudder says, crossing herself.

Angus nods and raises his teacup over the middle of the table. Pinky out, of course.

"God save us all. Now Mudder, as soon as we're done dinner, me and Hammy will make sure every drop of that demon brew is disposed of. I gives you my word."

I finally know why they call December twenty-sixth "Boxing Day." When I wake up, my head feels like it went twelve rounds with Muhammad Ali. I drag myself to the bathroom and drink water from the faucet. Ang appears in the mirror before I have a chance to look at my own face.

"Yep," he says. "I knew that was going to leave marks."

I notice for the first time the bruises on my forehead. When I raise my hands to the top of my head, there are bumps there. Something is wrong with the palms of my hands, too, the skin starting to peel, the sensation not all there. There's a similar feeling in my knees. I'm afraid to look at those.

Ang steps back and grabs the towel from the rack. He stands sideways and drapes the towel in front of me, flapping it like one of those fancy bullfighters in Portugal or wherever. "Toro! Toro!"

"What are you talking about? What happened to me?"

"You don't remember? Can't say I'm surprised. I was pretty much dragging you when you fell down and fought your epic battle with the garbage box."

My hands and knees all sting at once as I flash back to kneeling in the snow. Something big and hard is directly in front of me. The garbage box, I presume. I'm convinced the only way to move it is to butt it with my head.

"Best outdoor show I ever saw. You should write to the Calgary Stampede people. Tell them you have a new event."

"Fuck off, Angus."

He opens his mouth to make some comeback but gets cut off by Mudder wailing from the kitchen.

"Angus! Ambrose! The Mounties got poor little Wish."

We take off running. I almost bowl Mudder over as we slide to a halt on the waxed canvas floor. She points a shaking finger at the window. An RCMP cruiser is parked at the end of the lane. Constable Thornberry from across the Bay helps Wish out of the back seat, while some big cop I never saw before unloads Wish's toboggan from the trunk. Wish looks completely shit-baked as Thornberry pats him on the back and starts leading him toward the house. The big cop brings up the rear, toboggan under his arm.

"Maybe they're just giving him a ride home," Mudder says.

Ang shakes his head, eyes closed. "They wouldn't both get out of the car for that."

"Jesus, Mary and Joseph! What have you boys done?"

The door opens. Wish trudges straight to his room without a word, leaving the two Mounties crowding the doorway. As Mudder starts after Wish, the big cop leans the toboggan against the wall and nods my way. "Angus Pottle?"

"Ambrose."

"You don't have to tell them anything," Ang says, cool as a baloney sandwich.

Mudder stops at the closed door of Wish's room. She turns back to face the Mounties. "What have you done with my little boy?"

Constable Thornberry takes off his hat, solemn enough for a military funeral. "The lad is in no trouble, madam. All he did was return some beer bottles to the store. Six cases of Foster's Lager, to be precise."

"Sweet merciful shit," I hear myself saying. The last word comes out like a bird chirp as Ang stomps on my foot. The Mounties glare at us.

"You gentlemen need to come with us," says the big cop. "For questioning."

"About what?" Ang says. "You got nothing on us."

"We have probable cause to arrest you," Thornberry says, "but you can choose to come voluntarily."

"Shit." This time it's Ang.

We go voluntarily. It might be the last thing either of us does voluntarily for a while. The Mounties deposit us in the back seat of the cruiser, then hang back to talk to Mudder, who's screaming her head off at nobody in particular. So far, nobody seems to be looking at the shed.

"This is bullshit," I say. "It's not like those were the only cases of Foster's ever made. For all they know, I could have brought those back from Town months ago."

Ang stares straight ahead at the wire mesh separating us from the front seats, where the Mounties will be sitting in a few minutes. He rubs at his temples like he's warming up the machinery inside. When he finally speaks, his voice is calm and measured.

"Just stop, Hammy. The car is probably bugged."

I open my mouth to say how smart this is, then do exactly as Ang said. I stop.

"No need to panic," he says. "Her Majesty's ain't as bad as you think. You might even like it."

I look around for any kind of video equipment. Maybe a dash cam turned around to face the back seat. Satisfied there isn't one, I start mouthing words to Angus. *What are you talking about? What could I possibly like about jail?*

Ang leans back in the seat, doing his best to get comfortable. He turns and treats me to that grin of his. Something tells me he's been saving his next set of words for the perfect occasion.

"Fodder's in there," he says. "He'll be happy as a pig in shit to see you."

His words hit me like a sledgehammer to the face. I make no attempt to quiet my voice. "Our father?"

"Who art in custody," Ang replies.

"That's where he been all this time?"

"Yup. Don't tell Mudder, though. She's not supposed to know."

"Wow," I say. "Both of us together with Dad. Almost a shame to leave poor little Wish behind."

Ang shrugs. "Wish is still young. He'll get his chance."

"You think so?"

"I guarantee it, Hammy. With us as his role models, it's only a matter of time."

Honeymoon Sweet

Craig Faustus Buck

For a sweet house, right on Santa Monica Beach, it was unbelievably easy to break into. Mickey found a window he could open with a putty knife, so the double-locked doors were a joke. And Lana disabled the alarm within the forty-five-second grace period before it would have triggered. They were in and no one knew. What a great way to kick off the honeymoon.

Mickey couldn't imagine anything else they could have hijacked to bring them any closer to heaven: salt air, pounding surf, white sand, five-million-dollar love nest whose owner was en route to Europe. Lana had told him she'd always dreamed of a house on the beach and he'd delivered.

She strolled out of the alarm closet, clapping her hands to beat off the dust. Mickey's heart soared at his good fortune to have married her. He loved the sway of her hips, the trill of her laugh, the smell of her skin, how her jet-black bangs set off her turquoise eyes, the way she knew how to do things: clean a squid or repair a zipper or break down a Beretta. He'd known he wanted to marry her by their second date though he'd needed two months to muster the courage to ask.

He wrapped his arms around her and ran his tongue between her lips. She toyed with it for a moment, then yanked off his shirt. He pulled her sweater over her head. She slid her hand over his fly. He was already hard.

She stroked him through his pants as she backed him across the great room toward the wall of windows overlooking the moonlit Pacific. They knocked over a glass-shaded lamp but neither reacted when it shattered on the floor. She slammed him down on the couch and went straight for his belt buckle. He wrestled with her jeans. The heat was intense.

Their clothes were barely off, but he could already feel her tremble. This was record time for her, which only excited him more. Her tremors were intensifying, and he was along for the wild ride.

Then she froze.

Had he done something wrong? "What?" he said.

She put her finger to his lips, then whispered, "Didn't you hear that?"

He had not.

But then he did. Almost lost in the ocean's roar: *scritch scratch.* Like a mouse clawing at the inside of a wall. Someone was having trouble getting a key into one of the front-door locks.

They scrambled to pull on their clothes.

"I thought you said this place was going to be empty," said Lana.

"That's what Wally told me."

"Wally One-nut? You trusted that inbred idiot?"

Mickey knew he should have double-checked Wally's information. The guy was famous for blunders. But the deserted beach house had seemed so perfect that Mickey let romance cloud his judgment. Now, because of Wally's bad data, Mickey felt like a nitwit, a feeling he was getting to know all too well. That's what happens when you fall for a chick who's smarter than you. But did it have to happen on the first night of their honeymoon?

Scritch scratch.

Mickey crossed to the wall by the door, to be behind it when it opened. Lana rushed into the kitchen area, grabbed a chef's knife from the block and dropped out of sight behind the island.

The *scritch scratch* finally *clacked* as the key turned and shot the deadbolt.

As Mickey listened to the sound of the key moving to the second lock, the one in the door-handle that probably cost as much as his car, he felt the familiar rush of danger. That exhilaration was one of the main attractions of his line of work. He glanced toward the kitchen end of the great room and wished he could see Lana to share the anticipation. At least he knew she was there for him, knife in hand, ready to spring. *My wife has my back.* It had a nice ring to it.

The oversized door swung open, ramping up the sound of the crashing waves. A man stood framed in the doorway, stock still, as if sensing something wrong.

Behind the door, Mickey held his breath and peered through the spyhole. The fisheye gave him a funhouse-mirror view of the profile of the man. He was wearing a tuxedo and seemed off-balance as he turned to grab the huge stainless door handle. He now faced the spyhole and Mickey could see that he wore no tie or cummerbund. The waistband of his pants hung open, apparently to relieve the pressure of his slight pot belly.

The man headed back outside. *He knows we're here,* thought Mickey, *he's going for help.* Mickey was about to run after him when he heard the man throw up on the pavement in front. Mickey relaxed, flexing his hands to relieve his tension without making any noise.

The man stumbled back into the house and did a face-plant on the seagrass carpet. He lay on the floor like a sandbag, bathed in the blue moonlight reflecting off the ocean.

Mickey closed the door. Lana slowly approached the man and knelt to feel for a pulse.

"He's still breathing," she said.

"Let's get the fuck out of here," said Mickey.

"Give me a second."

She searched the man's pockets. He had a wallet, some keys, some breath mints and something that stopped her cold.

"Hello," she said and held up a glassine envelope filled with white powder.

"What is it?" he said.

Lana squeezed the sides of the envelope to pop it open. Dipping her little finger inside, she scooped a bit of the powder under her nail and touched it to her tongue. Her face scrunched up from the taste.

"Bitter," she said. "Not numbing like coke. I'm guessing smack."

She closed the packet, then grabbed a Kleenex from a nearby dispenser and wiped the glassine clean.

"What are you doing?" he asked.

"Hedging our bets."

Mickey had no idea what she was planning, but this honeymoon was clearly taking a sharp turn in a new direction.

Holding the envelope by its edges, she pressed the unconscious man's fingers onto the glassine. Then she wrapped the packet in the tissue and set it aside. Mickey was pleased that she hadn't pocketed the dope. He didn't think she did hard drugs, but this was the first time he'd seen her face the temptation.

She returned to her search. Mickey felt his anxiety building.

"It's time to go," he said. "If he comes around while we're here, we're talking felonies."

"Hang tight. This guy could be our ticket."

"You don't want to do hard time. Look what State prison did to your mother. You want to end up like her?"

Lana looked up empathetically. Mickey had met her mother soon after they'd gotten engaged. They'd picked the woman up at her halfway house and taken her to Denny's. When Lana went to the ladies' room, her mother offered to sell Mickey a happy ending after lunch. It had been an unpleasant afternoon for all.

"Babe," said Lana, "I promise you I'll never be like my mother."

She shuffled through the man's credit cards.

"Just take his wallet and let's blow."

She found a business card. "Avery Blain," she read. "Esquire. Beverly Hills law firm with six names and he's one of 'em." She held up another card. "Member of the Jonathan Club. This is looking more and more like a cash cow. And *we*, my blushing husband, are going to suckle the teats."

"Are you talking about selling that dope on the street?" he said.

"Please," she said contemptuously. He knew it was a put-down, but he didn't get it.

She fanned the contents of Avery's wallet like a poker hand, enticing him to pick a card. He reached out and plucked a photograph from the array.

It was a snapshot of a red-haired woman with an infectious smile posing beside a carousel horse. She was tall and well-padded but shapely, about Lana's age, maybe ten years younger than Avery Blain.

"You think this is his wife?" He flipped the photo for Lana to see.

They were startled by a loud belch and looked down at Avery, still lying with his face on the floor, his visible eye an amalgam of sky blue and rummy red. He stared at Lana's feet, but his expression implied no comprehension of what, much less whose, they were.

"You in or out?" asked Lana.

Mickey felt a fresh flush of excitement. He answered her question by stripping off his belt and binding Avery's hands behind his back. Their flirtation with felony had become a full-blown orgy. Life with this woman was going to be a kick.

Lana grabbed a dishtowel and tied it around Avery's eyes.

"Talk to him," said Mickey.

That was her job. Whenever they ran a scam, Lana did the talking. She was the one with the people skills.

She bent down and spoke softly in Avery's ear. "Can you hear me?"

He struggled against the restraint on his wrists.

"Relax, Avery," she said. "We're not going to hurt you. We just want to make sure you're calm before we talk. Okay?"

She patted his knee encouragingly.

"I just need to drop something off. I can't miss my flight."

She shot Mickey a glance then turned back to Avery.

"Where are you going?" she asked.

"My hands are stuck." He was still too groggy to grasp his situation.

"Doctor's orders. You've had too much to drink."

Mickey turned a chair around to watch Lana work. He straddled and crossed his arms over the back for a chin rest.

"I can't see," said Avery.

"If you want to make your flight, you'll have to trust me," said Lana. "Where are you flying?"

"Aix en Province" said Avery, pronouncing it "aches."

Mickey didn't know what the correct pronunciation was, but he was pretty sure this wasn't it. He asked, "Are you going alone?"

"Huh?" Avery turned toward the voice as if aware, for the first time, that a third person was in the room.

"He wants to know if you're meeting up with anyone in Aix en Province?" said Lana, pronouncing it "ex." Mickey suspected she knew. He felt a small burst of pride.

"What?" said Avery, struggling to shake off the booze.

"Maybe the woman whose picture you've got in your wallet?" she asked.

"She's divorcing me."

He let out a sob.

"Great," said Mickey. "A fucking basket case."

The disapproval in her glance irritated him.

"Why don't you do something helpful?" she said to Mickey. "Maybe find something we can use to get him upright."

She turned back to Avery and tenderly wiped his brow, chanting "It's okay" in a soothing voice, as if calming a child. A tear escaped the blindfold and dripped into Avery's ear.

As Lana tried to soothe Avery, she watched Mickey look through drawers and cabinets in the kitchen area. She felt bad about dismissing him like an underling, but he seemed unusually slow on the uptake and it annoyed her. Could it be that she'd never noticed how dense he was? Or was he folding under pressure? Apparently, she didn't know him as well as she'd thought.

They'd been together only six months, so his marriage proposal had come as a surprise. She'd been ambivalent. She couldn't decide if he was hopelessly romantic or deluded by lust. Joyfully spontaneous or dangerously impetuous. To his credit, the man's tongue was like a witching stick for her erogenous zones, discovering nerves she never knew existed, triggering feelings that turned her to jelly. And she was a sucker for the way his dark five-o'clock shadow set off his sweet baby face. Granted, he was no Rhodes scholar, but he made her laugh and he seemed sharp enough to avoid jobs that were likely to land him in jail.

Mickey pulled a roll of duct tape out of a catchall drawer and gave her a victory grin.

"Let's get old Avery off the floor," he said.

Mickey made Avery close his eyes, then swapped the dishtowel for duct tape wrapped around his head.

"Hey!" said Avery. "Watch the hair."

"I avoided your ears, didn't I?" said Mickey.

Typical male response, thought Lana. But Mickey was still better than most. For one thing, she felt certain he would never hit her. That just wasn't his style. And taking the fear out of love was nine tenths of the battle.

Mickey dragged an armchair over from the dining room table and helped Avery up and in. Then Mickey started taping.

"What the hell is going on here?" said Avery. He tried to kick but found his ankles strapped to the chair legs. He finally fathomed his predicament as Mickey wrapped the last strip around his calf.

"Who are you?" said Avery. "What do you want?"

"We want money, asshole," said Mickey. People skills be damned.

"Just take what you want and get out." said Avery. "All my cash is in my wallet."

"We don't want your petty cash," said Lana. "We want a payday."

"A big one," said Mickey.

"I don't negotiate with terrorists."

Avery sounded confident, as if he was used to dealing with thugs. Lana suspected he might practice criminal law.

"Well we don't take crap from junkies," said Mickey and slapped Avery's head hard enough to send him tumbling over in his chair. His head hit the mat carpeting with a sickening thud. It happened so fast it was over before Lana could react. Mickey shifted his weight to deliver a follow-up kick.

"That's enough!" she said, stepping between the two men. When she put her hand on Mickey's chest to hold him back, her fingers were trembling.

Mickey gave Avery a last look of contempt, then walked across the room to stare out the window. Lana watched him brood at the roiling black Pacific. She and Mickey had run plenty of cons together, and a few had gotten physical. The worst was the time they'd been caught by a rent-a-cop in a Brentwood mansion and Mickey had been forced to knock the guy down to get away. But that had been self-defense. This was the first time she'd seen him get aggressive. She felt something like indigestion in the pit of her stomach.

Lana tried to pull Avery upright, but the combined weight of the man and the chair were too much for her.

"A little help?"

Mickey came back and righted the chair. "Sorry," he said. To her, not to Avery. But she could tell Mickey's fury wasn't spent. His jaw was ticcing all over the place.

"Why don't you go downstairs," she said. "Find his investment records or bank statements. They'll either be in files or on his computer. Let me work my magic alone."

His fist clenched as he glared at Avery and she thought Mickey might try for one last shot. She was afraid she wouldn't be able to stop him. But then he turned and stomped down the stairs. Mickey was accustomed to two-bit swindles and low-risk burglaries. Kidnapping and extortion were much more serious crimes. She suspected the stakes were chafing his nerves.

Lana pulled a chair up close to Avery for an intimate conversation. She usually entered negotiations by trying to build a relationship with her mark. The blindfold made that problematic.

"How's your head?" she asked.

"Sobering fast," he said.

"Look. You're a named partner in a Beverly Hills law firm. I'm sure you've got a lot of high-powered friends and clients. You have a beautiful home on the beach in Santa Monica. You have a lot to lose. My husband and I understand it's in our interest to make this relatively painless for you. We're reasonable people. We don't want to take so much that you think it's worth a risk to try to get it back. We want your upside to be greater than your downside, so you're motivated to cooperate. We need your payout to be small enough that your lifestyle doesn't change because if anyone else finds out about your heroin hobby or our little agreement, who knows where that might lead? So, the idea is to make everybody happy, including you."

"I don't negotiate with terrorists," he repeated, but this time his voice lacked conviction. It was encouraging that the threat of exposure seemed to be weighing on him.

"We're not terrorists, Avery. Terrorists destroy things. We don't want to destroy you. We just want enough money to make us feel like our risk has been rewarded."

“If we go away happy, we'll go away forever.” She continued, “That's not terrorism. We don't want to destabilize anything. We're not anarchists, we're business people. You give us what we want, and you'll never see us again. Wouldn't that be the best solution all around?"

"The best solution would be for you to cut me loose and leave," he said.

She smiled. "If our relationship is going to work out, you need to face the truth about the situation you're in and be smart about getting out of it. Doesn't that make sense? Be honest with me."

"Honesty is a two-way street," he said. "You expect me to believe that lowlife husband of yours will just leave and not come back?"

Avery fidgeted against his bindings.

"Let me lay it out for you," she said. "You're a junkie. Which, I might add, is much more pathetic than being a lowlife."

"I'm no junkie. I'm an occasional recreational user."

"Spare me. What I have that you want is the incriminating evidence with your fingerprints all over it. What you have that I want is money--a fair price to make this all go away. Once I sell you the evidence, we'll have no leverage to come back at you with. You can shoot up your occasional recreation to your heart's content."

Lana was uneasy with the thought of abetting Avery's drug use, but if withdrawal was an unspoken bargaining chip, she wanted to make sure he understood that his dope was in the pot.

"That heroin isn't evidence of anything," said Avery. "If you call the cops, I'll just claim you brought it with you and forced me to put my prints on it. The D.A. won't even open a case."

"I'm not going to call the cops; I'll let some reporter do that. I'll send the dope to the *L.A. Times* as an unnamed addict who wants to come clean. I'll tell them my dealer is prominent Beverly Hills lawyer Avery Blain whose prints are all over the dope. They may be skeptical, but you can bet they'll follow up with the cops, the D.A., the State Bar, your partners, your friends and your neighbors. The publicity alone will kill your reputation. You can kiss your career goodbye, along with this house and your friends at the Jonathan Club. And if the cops find your dealer, you know he'll roll over and you'll go to prison."

They heard the crackling pop of splintering wood downstairs as if Mickey had crowbarred a locked drawer.

"He's looking for your financial records, Avery. That's step one in the simple resolution of this thing. I need you to show me how much you've got so we can settle on a figure and wrap this up quietly."

"My accountant has all my financials," he said.

Again, she felt hamstrung by the blindfold. Men lied easily with their words, but their eyes always gave them away.

"You're a lawyer, Avery. You're going through a divorce. That means you've been hiding assets. You're too smart to trust that to some accountant who might be called to testify under oath."

"There's nothing to hide. It's all tied up in the divorce."

Could he be telling the truth? Her bullshit meter was useless without seeing his eyes.

"Should I be worried about your wife walking in unannounced, Avery? It's better that I know. I'd hate for her to surprise us and wind up getting beaten up. You've seen how impetuous my husband can be."

"You don't have to worry about her," said Avery. "She wouldn't set foot in this house without a hazmat suit."

His lips quivered and she sensed his pain. Did they really need to blindfold him? She was certain she'd convinced Avery that they had him over a barrel.

Lana made a unilateral decision. She grabbed a pair of scissors from a pencil cup on the kitchen counter.

"Don't move," she said, and slipped a blade under the duct tape to cut through the band around his head. When she peeled it off his skin he winced.

She'd had a glimpse of his eyes before, but this was the first time she got a good look. The peek of blue she'd seen before was now revealed to be a dazzling multitude of shades, shimmering with the allure of a tropical lagoon. He returned her gaze and she felt him assessing her, like a jeweler examining a diamond through a loupe.

She tried to yank the tape off his hair, and he cried out in pain.

"My husband didn't give your blindfold a lot of forethought," she said.

"Forethought doesn't seem to be his long suit."

She had to cut through his hair to free it from the tape.

"I'm afraid you're going to need a buzz cut to fix this. Maybe shave your head."

The rhythmic white noise of the surf was suddenly pierced by the sound of a siren in the distance. Mickey came bounding up the stairs, looking frightened.

"Nobody knows we're here," she said. "Relax."

But he didn't. The siren grew louder.

And then it passed.

But relief was fleeting. "What the hell are you doing?" asked Mickey as he registered Avery's unmasking.

Lana's scissors were back under the duct tape, snipping at Avery's hair.

"What difference does it make?" she said. "He's not going to call the cops."

"He's a fucking witness!"

She didn't like being criticized, especially not by him. "He's got way more to lose from the cops than we do," she said. "Use your head."

"*You* use your head. What if his dealer finds out we hassled his customer? Avery can describe us. People can find us."

"You think I want anyone to find out about this?" said Avery. "You should listen to her."

Mickey's neck flushed crimson and he brandished his fist. "Listen to *this*, you lawyer fuck!"

Lana grabbed Mickey's arm to prevent him from swinging. He turned on her and she saw a feral rage in his eyes that chilled her. He was losing control under pressure.

She'd had bad luck with men like this in the past. The kind of luck that required hospitalization.

She felt something snap deep down inside and knew her trust in him had died. Her love for Mickey vaporized like a drop of water on a hot skillet.

Mickey went back downstairs to pick up where he'd left off--sweeping books off the wall-to-ceiling shelves in Avery's office, looking for a hidden safe.

Use your head. Was that supposed to be some sort of putdown? Because this whole snake pit was her idea. Mickey tried to brush a set of law books off a shelf, but they were too heavy, so he had to toss them on the floor one by one. One more pain in the ass to add to the list.

Use your head. This marriage thing was beginning to feel like a mistake. Maybe he'd been too hasty. He'd been so intoxicated by Lana that he'd wanted to strike while the iron was hot, before some other guy got his hooks into her. And then the honeymoon had started off with a bang. Even when Avery came along, they still seemed like they were riding high.

But now he wasn't so sure. He couldn't believe she'd cut off the blindfold.

Could she have a soft spot for Avery? The thought had been gnawing at Mickey since he'd seen her touch the guy. The only reason to touch someone you've got hogtied is to make them talk. And that entails pain. Yet she'd stroked his brow like a fucking nursemaid. She'd patted his knee. Did she think Mickey was blind?

He gritted his teeth and used all his strength to send thirty pounds of law books flying off the shelf.

Lana's mouth was dry from the adrenaline rush of Mickey's assault on Avery. She went into the kitchen to find something to drink. She was surprised when she opened the fridge. She'd expected a guy's fridge: beer, leftover pizza, bologna, ketchup, maybe something moldy and unidentifiable. But Avery's fridge was stocked with vegetables, fresh herbs, fancy stuff in jars. A guy who liked to cook. She'd never met one of those before. Mickey couldn't even open a can.

She walked back into the living room area with a Perrier, imagining Avery tipping a steak pan, letting the flames lick cognac fumes to light up a flambé. He wasn't a classically handsome man but there was something about him she found attractive. Fortyish, full head of silky black hair framed by graying temples, Grecian nose, and those eyes--kaleidoscopic blue and radiating intelligence, now that he'd sobered up a bit.

She cracked open the Perrier and took a sip.

She wondered what he'd be like in bed. She'd never been with a man who made his money legally. And never with one who made the kind of money you'd need to live right on the beach. She'd never known a life without the constant worry of being caught for one thing or another. Life with Avery would be a whole other ballgame.

"You must be thirsty," she said.

"A bit."

She held the bottle to his lips. He parted them and she poured slowly enough for him to drink. When he'd finished, she wiped an errant drop off his lip with her fingertip, then absently licked it off her finger. She watched his eyes follow her tongue.

"You really know how to pick 'em," he said. "What do you see in that jackass anyway?"

"He's just being cautious," said Lana. "Maybe too cautious. But we're newlyweds. He thinks he's supposed to protect me."

She could feel Avery's keen gaze boring into her innermost thoughts.

"You seem like the kind of woman who can take care of herself. Why would a woman like you want to haul around baggage like him?"

"You don't know anything about me," she said.

"Oh, but I do," said Avery. "I know you're already disillusioned with this marriage. I know your husband is already starting to irritate you. I know you think you could have done a lot better. And I know you still can."

She wondered how he could be so perceptive. He was a man, after all. Weren't all men emotional dolts?

She snipped the last of the tape away from his head. His hair looked like it had been vandalized.

"What about you?" she asked. "You say your wife hates you, but you cried when I asked about her."

"Booze tears don't count. I'm ready for a new beginning."

"You should take her out of your wallet," she said. "She's wasting space."

Mickey had looked everywhere downstairs for a safe. He'd checked for places where the carpet wasn't tacked down. He'd rapped his knuckles between the studs of every wall to make sure they were hollow. He'd scanned the ceiling for attic hatches. He'd pulled down every book and some pretty heavy art. He was frustrated and he was tired. Where the hell else would someone keep financial records?

As far as Mickey could see, Avery didn't have a computer and he didn't have a safe and he didn't have any files for investments or bank accounts. Could he be totally dependent on his smart phone? Mickey didn't think the financial dealings of a rich guy like Avery could be managed on a three-inch screen, but what did he know?

He stepped into Avery's office and flopped into the fancy mesh desk chair to regroup. He ran his finger across the hand-crafted bird's-eye maple trim that edged Avery's desk and felt something above the top of the right wall of the kneehole. It was a barely visible slit that he hadn't noticed when he'd first searched the room. He saw a matching slit on the left side. He reached between them and pulled on the trim. A hidden drawer slid out on glides, less than an inch deep, just big enough for Avery's MacBook.

Mickey smiled. Maybe he wasn't so stupid after all. He opened the notebook and watched it wake up. Avery's desktop resolved; no password required. The shmuck had assumed he was safe in his own home. Mickey felt a thrill of accomplishment in having shattered that complacency.

He clicked on a Wells Fargo icon and found himself staring at a login screen.

Lana watched Mickey top the stairs with a MacBook Air, grinning at her like a gladiator presenting his opponent's severed head to the Queen.

"Lookee what I found," he said. "Just need a few passwords from my buddy Avery."

"Change of plans," she said.

Mickey's face morphed from confusion to suspicion and back as she raised her arm. She was holding a gun--Avery's Glock--aiming at Mickey's heart.

"What the hell?" said Mickey.

"Surprise," said Avery. He lifted his hands. They were no longer taped to the chair. He swung his legs forward.

She had cut him free.

"You conned me into marrying you, Mickey," she said. "You pretended to be someone you're not."

"Baby, I love you."

"Honeymoon's over," she said. "I'm moving on."

"With him?" He shot Avery a sneer.

"Only losers slap people around for no reason," said Avery. "Smart women don't find that attractive."

Mickey's jaw was working overtime again. He looked at Lana. "You're dumping me for a fucking lawyer?"

She was enjoying Mickey's humiliation more than she'd thought she would. She gave Avery a lusty grin.

"I like a man who thinks things through," she said. "It makes me want to do dirty things."

Mickey erupted. ""You fucking bitch!" He launched himself at her.

Lana fired a shot into his chest.

Mickey went down. He took a labored breath and sucked air through his wound. She'd hit a lung. Mickey stared at her disbelievingly. His lips moved but he couldn't muster the strength to speak.

She felt unsettled. She'd never shot anyone before. She looked at Avery to make sure he'd caught it all on video. He gave her an assuring nod, then held the iPhone up for Mickey to see.

"You shouldn't have gotten violent," said Avery. "Now it's self-defense."

"See, Mickey?" She kissed her fingertips and touched them to Avery's lips. "He thinks things through."

"Go ahead," said Avery. "Finish the thought."

Lana pointed the Glock at Mickey's forehead and fired again.

She stared at Mickey's corpse as the relentless pounding of the ocean slowly washed the gunshot's echo from her ears.

"Till death do us part," she said.

Avery wiped his own prints off the packet of heroin, knelt beside Mickey and pressed the dead man's fingerprints onto the glassine. Then he slipped the envelope into Mickey's pocket.

"Here's what we tell the police," said Avery. "You were unhappy in your new marriage, so you went for a walk on the beach to think about it. I saw you and struck up a conversation. When you found out I was a lawyer you asked if I knew anything about annulments. I invited you up to discuss it. Your husband must have been following you. He barged in, raving like a lunatic. I tried to get the gun I keep in the sideboard, but he jumped me, and it fell. He knocked me down and dove for the gun, but you grabbed it first. He threatened to kill you and I started a phone video in case you wanted to press charges. That's when he attacked you. You were afraid for your life. You had to shoot him."

"So much to remember."

"I'll do the talking. As your attorney, I'll advise you not to speak."

They heard the wail of an approaching siren.

Someone must have heard the shots.

Lana stared out at the crashing waves reflecting the moonlight like small explosions of neon white. A tear rolled down her cheek. She'd always dreamed of a life on the beach.

Work At Home Opportunity! Perfect for Single Moms

Laurie Zottmann

Chucky Jensen pulls up in front of the dingy pub and her headlights glint off a crack in the window. The sight of that silver ribbon makes her sweat inside her parka. She's done bad things in the booth behind that crack. Tonight, she's here to do another.

She pops her door and it catches on the wind that's barreling like a buffalo through the empty lot. The door hinge screams and the panel *thwongs* into an aluminum pole. One with a handicapped parking sign on top.

Chucky groans. She gets out shoves the door closed with her butt. As she reaches around to wipe the road grime off her coat, a bright light blinds her.

She shades her eyes as a huge SUV pulls in beside her. Blinking, she takes in the vehicle: a coat of arms on a white door. A light bar on top.

Fuck me! She thinks.

The passenger window whirrs down.

"Can't park here, Chucky," says a familiar voice.

"I *know*, Matt," she says. "I was just moving."

"Were you?"

She grits her teeth. "I said I was, *Officer*. Don't you have something better to do? Like searching for missing husbands?"

In the shadows, she can't see his face, but she knows Matt's furrowing his Cro-Magnon brow.

"I don't know, Chucky," he finally says. "Seems like a waste. I'm bettin' dollars to donuts, all we need to do is dig up your backyard."

Her heart jumps. She touches her throat and mutters to herself.

"What was that?"

"I said, *get a warrant, asshole.*" She spins on her heel and stomps through the foot-deep snow up to the sidewalk. She has her hand on the thick brass door handle, but she pauses.

"Fuck." She spins back around, stomps back to her car, and moves it over one space. Matt's already gone.

Inside the pub, it's dark and grubby. Chucky pulls her hood back. There's only one customer: in his sixties, slouched over a half-empty pint glass at the bar. His head bobs toward the hockey game.

The kitchen door squeaks. There's Andy. Chucky's tongue sticks in her throat. She hasn't seen him in four years, but her Bad Thing brother-in-law looks exactly the same. Ex-brother-in-law, now.

"Hey, kid," he says, smirking. "I knew you couldn't stay away."

Her heart beats way too fast. "You said you had a line on a job."

"Sure did!" Andy grins. "Got something for you in back. Come on." He turns and heads toward the kitchen.

She holds back.

He looks over his shoulder and rolls his eyes. "I'm not putting a gun to your head, Chuck."

She follows.

Andy leads her through the kitchen, past the dull stainless glow of the prep station and the flattop with its greasy-gold patina. A wall of smells presses against them: skunky notes of old canola clashing with the bleach wafting up from grout that never forgets a scandal.

The odours suck Chucky back to the grim years of her youth: falling asleep in school and hustling tables by night. Keeping the lights on in the trailer she shared with her drunk dad. In grade eleven, she traded him in for Danny, the captain of the football team. He promised to take care of her.

They quit school a month before graduation and he started a landscaping business. They bought a dumpy house and she scrubbed at stains in the carpet older than she was. He worked late. She got pregnant and named the baby

Lenore. Then she found out Danny was humping his teenaged assistant.

They fought. He said he'd quit. But he didn't. Chucky made a choice: calcify her heart, focus on her daughter, and teach her to make better choices. She also fucked Danny's brother. But just the once.

Then she found out about the debts.

Chucky didn't know what to do when Vinnie and Lou showed up at the door. They asked for Danny, who by some magic premonition had been suddenly compelled to run out for beer. The big men stepped inside and looked around. They complimented their beautiful home, their tv, their vehicle. Winked at their beautiful baby girl. Chucky clutched Lenore to her chest and watched wordlessly as the thugs exchanged a look and left. She knew they'd be back.

Danny brushed off her furious questions and told her not to worry. Chucky squeezed her eyes shut and soldiered on. She couldn't force the truth out of him. Couldn't make him stop twisting the noose around her neck. She was powerless, at the mercy of his stupidity.

But on long nights, when the baby was teething and Danny didn't come home, she'd fantasized. Duct taping Danny to his weight bench, pouring Drano down his throat, and watching him puke blood until his stomach turned inside out. It had been a comfort.

In real life, the goons kept circling. Bad things happened.

Now, Chucky's a single mom with a double mortgage. Square one. Minus one.

Her stomach drops when Andy stops beside the dishwasher. “I can’t be your dishpig,” she says. “I’ve got no one to watch Lennie at night. I just… I can’t.”

Andy squeezes her shoulders. “Haven’t I always looked out for you, Chuck? Shut up and let me show you what we’ve got.” He grabs her hand and pulls her past the walk-in fridge.

His fingers are warm. Smooth. Impossibly familiar.

Chucky shakes off a jolt of hunger. *It was a lifetime ago,* she thinks. *It isn’t anything.* But the stress has her body on high alert. And Andy’s neck looks so touchable. Lickable. She can hardly breathe. Would he be standing there, so willing, if he knew what she’d allowed to happen?

Andy glances back at her, like he felt the flush of heat in her palm. He grins. Then he leads her into the yellow hallway. It gets darker as they go, and stinkier. Soon, the unmistakable tang of restaurant dumpster burns her throat. At the door, Andy squeezes her hand and pops the latch bar with his hip. It opens onto the loading dock.

A gust of wind swirls around them, and Chucky shivers in her coat. A thought pokes at her brain: *what if Andy wants revenge?* Most people don’t believe the rumours, and Andy’s a sweet, trusting guy. But still.

Andy steps close and leans into her ear. “How’d you like to become a down-low sales rep for the Sweet Cheeks corporation?”

“You want me to pimp little kids?”

Andy recoils. “Jesus fuck, what?”

"I don't know! You wouldn't say anything over the phone, then you drag me out here to the *perfect* kill zone, and I'm suddenly *hyper*-aware of the fact that I'm desperate enough to get roped into a fucking nightmare!"

"Sweet lords of neurosis," he mutters.

Angry tears slide down Chucky's face. Andy hands her a napkin. She fills it with a blow and folds it up to wipe her face. She takes a big breath and lets it out.

"All right?" he asks.

"All right," Chucky says.

Andy claps his hands and sprints around the back of the bin. A moment later, he returns, backing into view pulling a pallet jack. It's loaded with cardboard boxes. He does his best Vanna White arms.

"You, my friend, have just acquired a misplaced shipment of premium women's yoga pants."

Chucky's jaw swings like a dog door in the wind. What the fuck am I supposed to do with an assload of lycra?

Andy shakes his hands at her. "This shit is like *crack* to yuppy moms, Chuck! You're gonna be *swimming* in green!"

Chucky looks down at her own second hand, no-name jeans. She looks up again. Shrugs. "O-kaaay. But… where the fuck did you...?"

Andy puts a finger to her lips. "Don't ask. Just say thanks."

The next morning, Chucky sits at the kitchen table. She's scrolling on her laptop and sipping a tea when six-year-old Lenore pads into the kitchen.

"Mommy?" Lennie croaks, rubbing her eyes.

Chucky says, "Wow, you're up early."

Lennie yawns. "I had to pee, and I couldn't get back to sleep."

Chucky ruffles her girl's hair. "Me too, kiddo. Want some breakfast?"

Lennie doesn't answer, just presses her back against her mother's chest. Chucky strokes her hair with one hand and keeps scrolling with the other.

Lennie's little eagle eyes follow along. "What's multi-level markering?"

"Marketing, my love. And it means paying somebody lots of money so you can help them sell things."

Lennie screws up her face. "You have to pay money to work for somebody?"

"Yup. Crazy, right?"

Lennie nods, eyes wide. "Is that why you don't have a job, Mommy? Because we don't have the money to buy you one?"

Chucky swallows a lump in her esophagus. "Well… I have a job now. I'm going to sell leggings."

"Oooo!" Lennie says, clapping her hands. "Can I have some pink ones, with purple stars, and silver sparkles? Mandy in my class has some like that, and they are so cool!"

Chucky sighs. “I’m sorry, Sweetie. These leggings are just for grown-ups.”

Lennie’s face crumples.

“But when we finish selling them, we’ll find out where Mandy got hers, and we’ll get your very own pair, okay?” Chucky says.

Lennie cocks a suspicious eyebrow. “Not Value Village ones, right Mommy? I want my very own *brand*-new pair with *all* the glitter still on!”

“Deal,” Chucky says, wondering, How much are those things gonna cost?

Lennie squeals like a delighted piglet and squeezes her mom around the neck. Chucky coughs, but the long-lost sparkle in her daughter’s eyes is worth it.

A few days later, Chucky opens her email to see a note from Lennie’s school: “Thank you for registering a table at our Parent Market Fundraiser.”

“...the fuck?” Chucky mutters as she clicks on the subject line.

Inside the message it says:

Dear Parent Market Seller,

We have received your sign-up form to rent a table at our St Patrick's Day Market. You've been assigned a numbered table to display your merchandise:

- Charlene Jensen
"Leggings Just for Grown Ups" - Table #0023

See the .pdf map to find out where your table will be situated.

**** **Please Note:** You must pay the $75 registration fee within 48 hours to confirm your registration. We can accept payment via the board of education website. If you need to pay by cash or cheque, please see Donna in the school office during regular hours.*

Thank you for donating your time and profits for this event! We hope to raise the final $5,000 to repair the leaking skylights over the library.

With gratitude,

Your Parent Council

"Lenore!" Chucky shouts. "Get your butt in here!"

In the living room, the toy piano stops crashing. Then Lenore skids into the kitchen "What, Mommy?"

"What the hell is this Parent Market shit?"

"Oh! I signed you up!" She turns to Chucky, flushed with pride. "Ms. Johnson helped me. We're gonna raise lots of money and get new bean bag chairs in the library!"

"Baby, I don't think I can…"

"The old bean bags got stinky," Lennie interrupts. Her eyes get wide and serious. "They made sprouts." Lennie frowns. "But not the eating kind. I asked."

Chucky chuckles and sighs. “Honey, you can’t sign me up for things without telling me. I’m not sure if I can do that market thing.”

“But Mommy, you have to! You don’t have any stars on the parent volunteer chart!”

“There’s a parent volunteer chart?” She tries to remember the last time she read the class newsletter.

Lennie nods. “Every week we share something our family does to make the world better.”

“Every week? Jesus Christ.”

Lennie’s mouth squiggles to the side. “Sonia Bell made this huge poster that her dad printed on shiny paper, with pictures of her family’s mission in Guatemala. They’re super proud because they built a school out of mud, or something.”

Chucky hides her chuckle with her hand.

“So… I told everyone that I really miss my daddy… because he went to Africa with Hermione from Harry Potter.”

Chucky stops chuckling.

“Ms. Johnson said that was *amazing*. She showed us pictures on the internet of Hermione with short hair and talked about the United Playstations.”

Chucky slaps her forehead.

“The second week,” Lenore continues, “I said daddy and Hermione built a school to teach girls how to have a business. Just like daddy’s landscape truck!” Lenore looks at the floor as her cheeks pinken. “And then the third week, I told my class they were teaching everyone in the village how to read with the Harry Potter books." Lennie stops and swallows. "But then my tummy started to hurt." She buries her face in Chucky's shoulder and howls. "Ms. Johnson made me take our stickers off the parent volunteer chart!"

Chucky rocks her girl, with tears in her eyes and magma in her gut. "I'm going to make everything better, Sweetheart. I promise."

Later, when Lenore's in bed, Chucky massages her temples. Seventy-five dollars? She thinks. I'll have to sell a bunch of these thrice-damned things before I can even pay for the stupid registration. Then her eyes get wide. Jesus assfucking Christ. How am I going to find people who want to buy stolen leggings?

The next afternoon, Chucky's phone pings with another email from the school.

"Don't forget - 24 hours left to register your table!"

"Ugh," Chucky grunts, and pushes her phone across the table. She chews at the shredded skin around her nails. *Where the fuck am I going to come up with $75 for the table?*

Her phone chimes again, this time an alarm. "Pickup time."

In the hallway outside the classroom, Chucky picks at her cuticles and looks longingly at the huddle of cool moms. They're commiser-bragging about their prize-pet children's overpriced jazz recitals.

"Seven hours!" one mom snarks. "Our pre-recital picture day took seven. Freaking. Hours!" Her heavily defined eyebrows arch in a perma-snarl.

"I knooooow!" cooes another woman. "Miss Cheryl *insisted* that we show up at 7am, even though the photographer wasn't even booked until 8:30."

"Oh, God!" gasps another mom, gesturing with nails as bright as Skittles. "We got Aurora up at 5:30am! It took *forever* to do her mascara. And *then* we couldn't find her hair piece!" She throws her talons in the air. "You should have heard me yell."

In her eavesdropping corner, Chucky's chin hits her chest. She expects the women to exchange awkward glances, but to her horror, they all nod at Skittles.

"Tough love," says a tall mom dressed head-to-toe in Lulu Lemon. "Our mothers didn't coddle us, thank Jesus."

"Amen!" the women chorus.

Chucky's cheeks burn. She wrenches her stare away from the coven and locks onto the baseboards across the hallway.

It's almost let-out time. More mommies and nannies file into the hallway. Chucky's focus blurs as their lower bodies glide through her field of vision. Brand-name jeans, power suit pants, and leggings with mesmerizing patterns strut past her on confident, well-maintained thighs. Chucky's head snaps up.

Leggings!

She counts three pair of spandex-clad cameltoes floating into orbit around the It Moms. Four more on the sharp-taloned bitches themselves.

Jackpot!

"Uhm… Hey!" Chucky shouts, shoving off from her slouch on the wall. "Does anybody here buy leggings?"

Seven perfectly-glossed mouths fall open and stare at her like she just crawled out of the garbage. The silence stretches for a heartbeat. Then two. Chucky's hopeful smile falters.

One of them laughs. "Um, yeah! We all get our Sweet Cheeks from Tammy's parties. Weren't you at the Christmas one? It was a fundraiser for the classroom."

Chucky's face goes from egg-frying temperature to tin-smelting. "Oh, right! Haha. Yeah," she sputters. "I was just… ah… wondering… where I could get some more? For my legs?"

The mom posse stares viciously.

"Fuck me," Chucky mutters, pressing the heels of her palms into her eye sockets.

"What's that, dear?" Says a kindly voice at her shoulder. It's old Mrs. Harris.

"Oh! Nothing," Chucky answers, trying to return the sturdy woman's warmth. "I was just saying… ah… 'Lucky me!' I just got a new job."

"Good for you, dear," Mrs. Harris says, patting Chucky's hand. "A little independence does wonders for the libido!" She winks and chuckles at Chucky's dumbstruck expression. Then she shuffles off.

"A-hem."

Chucky turns to the pissy voice to see Tammy Mitchell's face pressed up into hers. She's so close, Chucky can see the tiny knots in Tammy's eyelash extensions.

"Listen, Trailer Park," Tammy breathes. "There's only room for one legwear distributor in this community. These bitches are mine. So, if you've gone and sold your TV or something to get the Petite Derierre starter kit, you're going to have to crawl back to the 'hood to sell them." She steps back with a lemon juice smile and waves her middle finger.

That evening, Chucky plunks Lennie in front of Netflix and "Barbie, Life in the Dreamhouse," the most annoying production on the planet, which she saves only for child-minding emergencies. Then she takes a deep breath.

She shuffles into the bathroom with the light turned off and dials her phone with a sweaty hand.

"S'up, Chuck?" Andy says.

Chucky swallows. "Um… you know the leg-"

Andy coughs loudly into the receiver. "Not on the phone."

Chucky makes a couple of gaping fish-mouth movements before she understands. "Oh! right. Um. You know, the thing… we talked about?"

"Uh-huh,"

"Well, um… I need a little… help. To get started."

“Whaddya need?”

Chucky breathes deep. “About seventy-five? By lunchtime tomorrow?”

Andy chuckles. “Why not make it an even hundred? I know you’re good for it.”

Chucky’s guts squirm.

“I’ll be there before breakfast,” Andy says.

“Okay,” Chucky whispers.

“You can call me again, you know,” Andy says. “Just for coffee, or something.”

“Okay,” Chucky repeats, while the panic swells. How do people ever get far enough ahead their sins to plan a date?

“I’ve always got your back, kid. Remember that.” Then Andy hangs up before Chucky starts to cry.

The next morning, Chucky stands at the school secretary’s desk with four smooth twenties when her phone pings with an email notification. “Parent Market Deadline is NOON today!”

She grins and signs the registration form with a proud flourish.

Chucky’s soaring confidence takes a nose-dive on market day when she sees the other tables getting set-up. Custom-branded tablecloths, stand-up banners, and literature trays with business cards and brochures shouting about opportunities to join dynamic sales teams.

Her bra suddenly feels too tight.

"Need some help?" asks a deep, familiar voice behind her. Chucky turns around and her stomach drops into her boots.

Matt.

"Um... ah..." Chucky stammers. "No! Ah, god. I mean... no, thanks, Matt. Thanks. I'm good."

Matt scowls at her, like he always does. Then he shrugs and walks away.

Chucky watches him go. Her knees buckle. She catches herself on her table. Then she lurches out of the gymnasium and around the corner into the girl's room. She slams herself inside a stall, bolts the lock, and sinks onto the shin-high toilet seat. She whips out her phone.

"SOSOSOSOSOSOSOSOSOSOS!!!!"

"???" Andy answers.

"Matt's here! And I have no biz cards. Or flyers. Or any trappings of legitimacy AT ALL!!!"

"Hang on," he types back.

Chucky clutches her chest and waits.

An eternity later, she gets a text from an unknown number. "Pack it up," it says.

"Who is this?" Chucky writes.

"Get THE FUCK out of there." the mystery messenger answers. "NOW, Chucky."

Chucky claps her hand over her mouth and whispers. "It's the fucking mob!"

"Mrs. Jensen?" a concerned voice shouts, echoing off the tiles. "Are you in here?"

Chucky wipes her eyes with her fingers. "Yes!" she says. "I'm here."

"It's me, Donna. The secretary? I'm sorry to intrude. Just wanted to make sure you're okay, because someone said you dashed in here looking sick."

"Oh!" Chucky shouts. "Yes! Yes, I am. I'm very sick. I have to go home. Right now."

"Oh, dear," Donna says. "Of course." Then after a pause, "Do you want me to man your table? I told a ton of moms that you were selling, and they're really excited to buy from you!"

Chucky's mouth moves silently. Her mind spins.

Donna's sensible leather shoes tap quietly toward Chucky's stall, and stop in front of her door. Through the crack, Chucky can see her lean in. "Just between us," Donna whispers, "we're all excited to deal with someone other than Tammy Mitchell."

Chucky's eyes widen in horror. "Tammy's selling here?"

"Mmm-hmm," secretary says quietly. "And she sells great stuff. But… you know. She's a little…"

"Vicious?" Chucky whispers, clutching her throat.

"Yeah," Donna answers. There's a beat of silence. "So, you want me to run your table?"

Chucky groans. Her stomach cramps. "Um… no, Donna. But… thank you. For the offer. I just… don't have my… credit card thingie… to set up for you."

"Ah," Donna says. "Of course. Well, let me at least help you pack up."

"Okay," Chucky says. "Just give me a minute."

"No problem!" Donna chirps, and she steps lightly out of the bathroom.

When Chucky gets to her table, it's empty. No cardboard boxes full of illicit wedgie-wear. Her heart leaps into her throat.

"Over here!" Donna shouts, waving from the emergency exit door. She swings the door open onto the parking lot. "Short cut!"

Chucky gives her a strained smile and speed-walks across the gym. She hip-checks someone on her way by, but doesn't stop to apologize.

Donna presses the door open wider and a gust of fresh air hits Chucky's face just as she collides with Tammy Mitchell.

"Oh my god!" Chucky sputters.

Tammy straightens her not-at-all displaced cardigan and gives Chucky an icy smile. "Everything's been straightened out. Take care of that stomach, *Chucky.* I hear there's a bad bug going around that's just *ruining* people."

Chucky gapes like a suffocating fish as Tammy struts off, chin in the air.

She glances desperately at Donna, who waves warmly. "Tammy offered to help me load your stuff. You're all set! Go home and feel better, Chucky. And give your cutie pie a hug for us!"

Chucky waves back numbly, then zombie-walks to the back of her car to close the hatch. Her four boxes are stacked tightly in there, with a note scribbled smearily in what looks like brown-black eyeliner. YOU'RE DEAD, TRAILER PARK, it says.

Chucky's head snaps up. She catches a glimpse of Tammy whispering in Matt's ear just as the gym door clicks shut.

Not knowing where else to go, Chucky drives aimlessly for over an hour before heading home. She parks in her own garage with a trunk full of stolen merchandise which has most likely just been reported to the police.

"Fuck. Fuck. Fuck!" she hollers, banging her head on the steering wheel. In response, her text ringer buzzes.

Chucky snatches up her phone and is shaking so hard, she fucks up the password three times before she can finally read the message.

"Go inside," says the mystery number. "NOW. Stall him."

Stall who? Chucky throws her door open and bangs it against Danny's stand-up tool chest. She grabs her purse and phone and lunges out of the garage and across the back lawn. She scrabbles at the back door with her key, babbling unintelligible curses, and tears stream down her face.

Just as she shoulders the door open, she hears heavy footsteps on the front porch. The doorbell rings.

Chucky moans and bounces on the balls of her feet. She stumbles through the kitchen and living room. Snaps the lock and twists the handle, then opens the door a tiny crack. It's Matt.

"I need to come in, Chuck."

Chucky opens the door, contorting her face into a gassy-looking smile.

Matt steps past her and looks around, stone-faced. "Do I need to search your garage, Chucky?"

Chucky's mouth suddenly has no spit. "Um… uh…" She swallows. Licks her lips. It just gets stickier in there. *Stall him…* "Search for what?"

"You really want a bunch of cops with a warrant rummaging through this place?"

Chucky shakes her head and Matt shakes his, shouldering past her, clomping across the hardwood in his dirty boots.

Chucky vaguely thinks, *Don't wake up Lennie,* but then she remembers Lennie's staying at a friend's tonight. Thank Jesus.

She follows Matt through the kitchen in a trance. He lets himself out the back door and marches across the yard. He doesn't look back at her until he reaches the garage door.

"Is it open?" he asks.

Chucky nods silently.

Matt turns the handle and pushes the door open. Chucky's feet have bonded with the paving stones. They're going to have to chisel her out of here to haul her off to jail.

Oh, Jesus Christ, she thinks. Who's going to take care of my kid?!?

The light in the garage flicks on. Chucky hears clicks and slams as Matt opens each door of her car. She counts them out: One. Two. Three. Four… Five.

The light clicks off, and Matt emerges into the night. Chucky hugs herself, shivering in the February wind. Matt looks her in the eye and stalks up to her.

"What's in the hole, Chuck?"

"H-h-hole?" Chucky rotates her neck slowly, following Matt's thumb toward the snow-covered lump she's managed to forget about at the base of her deck. But it's not snow-covered anymore. It's fresh-turned. A whoosh of dizziness swirls in Chucky's brain. Suddenly, she really has to pee.

Matt steps in closer. Chucky can smell the onion rings on this breath.

"I said," Matt growls, his Cro-Magnon unibrow folding in annoyance, "what's in that fucking hole, Chucky?"

Chucky smacks her lips. "I don't know," she rasps. It's all she can think to say. She physically cannot force herself to confess her sins to her disgusted neighbour cop.

Matt clenches his fists at his sides. Then he breaks his silverback gaze and stomps through the crusted drifts to lean over the hole.

He scrubs his thick hands over his face. Then he clenches his teeth and turns on her. "You know you need a permit to lay pipe to heat the garage?" He brushes past her and storms up the back steps. "And a professional, before you blow your ass up."

With his hand on the doorknob, he turns back. "Jesus, woman. Can't you just..." He looks at the sky, his face crinkling like he's in pain. "Can't you ever make things easy on yourself?"

A sob bubbles up from Chucky's belly. She buries her face in her hands. "What the fuck does that mean?"

There's no answer.

Chucky looks up. Matt's gone. The back door is open, and through the hallway she can see him letting himself out the front. He closes the door behind him softly, without looking back.

Her phone buzzes.

"Looks like you need some landscaping," says mystery number. "I used to know a guy."

Chucky gasps as her heart spasms. Her phone buzzes again.

"Don't worry, kid," it says. "We'll figure something out. I've always got your back."

Sex Toys

Michael Bracken

Darrell and Bocephus Taylor — half-brothers on their father's side and first cousins on their mothers' — sat at Darrell's yellow Formica kitchen table drinking Mountain Jack, a combination of Mountain Dew and Jack Daniel's. Seven years older than Bocephus, Darrell moved to Dallas five years earlier and supported himself with minimum wage jobs and petty crime. Bocephus was fresh off the bus from Redemption, a barely-there town in West Texas, sent to live with his older brother after their father began taking an interest in the third and youngest Heatherton sister.

A week before Bocephus's arrival Darrell stole a briefcase containing a folder of worthless legal documents and a 9mm Glock. When leaving the bus station after collecting his younger brother, he stole a purse containing thirteen dollars and an unloaded .32-calibre revolver. He took both events as a sign he was destined for greatness and that his younger brother was the key to his success. Tired of stealing bicycles and baby strollers, Darrell had ambition, and through an ever-thickening Jack Daniel's haze, he outlined his plans.

"We're going to start by knocking over Naughty Betty's," Darrell said, and explained to his younger brother that Naughty Betty's was an adult boutique located at one end of a strip mall.

"What are we going to steal?" Bocephus asked. "A bunch of dirty magazines?"

Darrell slapped the back of his half-brother's head. "It's pretty much a cash business," he said. "Who wants a record of them buying sex toys?"

Bocephus smoothed down the mussed-up portion of his finger-length hair and took another swig of Mountain Jack from his jelly jar. He still wore the red and gray letterman jacket he'd worn during the entire trip from Redemption, and he peeled it off to reveal a yellowing wife-beater. He also wore tight, faded Wrangler's and well-worn brown cowboy boots. Except for their apparel, Bocephus could have been Darrell's clone—same lithe build, same sun-blond hair, same blue eyes, and, inherited from their father, the same prominent nose that some mistakenly believed indicated endowment below the belt. They also shared the same smirk, and Bocephus smirked at his older brother. "How we going to do it?"

"Destiny was in there the other day, and she said Naughty Betty works alone." Destiny, a bleach blonde who often wore more make-up than clothing, expected Darrell to provide her with the finer things in life — Marlboro Lights, Shiner Bock, and weekend shopping trips to Sam Moon — in exchange for her amorous attentions. "I've been watching Betty's ever since, and it gets lots of traffic on Friday and Saturday nights."

"So, we go in, scare the old lady, and she gives us all the money, is that it?"

Darrell slapped the back of his brother's head a second time.

"I got to go in there and look the joint over," Darrell said. He upended the Jack Daniel's bottle and watched the last of it drip into his jelly jar of Mountain Dew. "I need to know if there're any video cameras or alarms or anything."

Thursday evening, Darrell convinced Destiny to take him to Naughty Betty's by promising to buy her the sex toy of her choice. They were sitting at his kitchen table while Bocephus sat in the living room watching a rerun of *Cops,* the television volume battling with his running commentary. "Why you running, fool? You know they're gonna get you!"

"What about your brother?" Destiny asked. "Doesn't he want to come, too?"

"We'd best leave him at home," Darrell said.

Destiny cut a glance at the younger Taylor and wet her lips with the tip of her tongue. "That's a shame."

"He'll just get in the way."

"Not if we do it right."

"Get your purse," Darrell said. "We can stop at Betty's on the way to your place."

Bocephus didn't look up from the television until Darrell opened the apartment door and Destiny stepped into the hall. "Where you guys going?"

"I'm taking Destiny home," Darrell said. "Don't wait up."

Bocephus had been downing Mountain Jack all night and it was just as likely the caffeine would keep him awake, as it was the alcohol would put him to sleep. "Don't do anything I wouldn't do."

Darrell shook his head and closed the door behind him as he stepped into the hall. He caught Destiny's arm, walked her downstairs and outside to his Ford F-150, and within half an hour parked at the strip mall outside Naughty Betty's. The blacked-out windows on the end unit prevented him from seeing inside, so he wasn't certain what to expect when he stepped into the adult boutique. He was temporarily distracted from his primary mission when he saw the plethora of sex toys cram-packed into the shop.

"You didn't tell me about all of this," he whispered to his girlfriend as their trek through the relatively innocent displays of edible underwear and sexy card games at the front of the shop led to ever-more-specialized accessories.

He knew about crotchless underwear because Destiny owned several pairs, and he knew about dildos and vibrators and flavored lube, but as a vanilla sex guy he was not prepared for the towering displays of butt plugs, cock rings, and nipple clamps. Nor had he anticipated the variety of ticklers, paddles, and whips; ball gags, masks, and handcuffs; black vinyl hoods, hogtie sets, and other bondage gear.

Destiny sashayed to the back of the shop and showed him the selection of strap-ons. Darrell did not comprehend why she wanted one — his equipment worked perfectly fine, thank you very much — but he pointed to one with a pink attachment. She took the box from the shelf and carried it to the front counter, where Naughty Betty stood waiting.

"This all for you?" Naughty Betty asked in a deep, sultry voice. She used spackle for make-up and dressed liked Darrell's grandmother, in a blue cotton-print dress, her gray hair lacquered into a helmet, and her white cat's eyeglasses dangling from a chain around her neck.

An old-fashioned cash register occupied the center of the counter, and on either side of it were a black leather punishment paddle with a solid metal core and a selection of handcuffs. While Destiny examined the handcuffs, Darrell looked for security cameras. He didn't see any, but he did notice the handwritten sign taped to the wall behind Naughty Betty.

Special Orders Filled

Unable to imagine anything the shop didn't already have on display, Darrell pointed at the sign, asking, "What kind of special orders? What do people order?"

"You'd be surprised at the things people like to do to each other," Naughty Betty explained with a suggestive smile. "But we fill every order."

Destiny selected a pair of plush love cuffs and put them on top of the strap-on box.

"Anything else?"

"I forgot the lube. What do you recommend?"

Naughty Betty stepped from behind the counter and walked Destiny to a display rack. While they discussed the various products, Darrell continued to examine the shop. The only three doors — the entrance, one that led into a restroom, and one that led into the storage room — seemed easy enough for Bocephus to watch while Darrell dealt with Naughty Betty and emptied the cash register.

Destiny and Naughty Betty returned with a bottle of lube, the older woman rang up their purchase, and Darrell paid with cash. Then he took Destiny to her apartment and, after she handcuffed him to her bed, learned exactly why she wanted the strap-on.

Bocephus looked up from the television when his brother opened the door and walked gingerly into the apartment. "What happened to you?"

"I don't want to talk about it."

Bocephus followed Darrell into the kitchen. "Did you look the place over?"

"Yeah. I did."

"And?"

Darrell leaned against the kitchen sink, opened a bottle of Jack Daniel's, and took a long swig that made him cough and spew a mist of alcohol across the kitchen. He took another long swig and said, "Saturday night, just before closing."

Most of the businesses in the strip mall closed early Saturday evening, leaving open only Naughty Betty's at one end and a faux Irish bar at the other end, far enough away that most of the bar's patrons paid no attention to the comings and goings at Naughty Betty's.

Darrell and Bocephus waited in Darrell's F-150 until the last customer exited the adult boutique at five to midnight before pulling on their masks, a pair of Destiny's black fishnet pantyhose cut in half to create matching stocking masks. Darrell took the .32-calibre revolver from the reusable shopping bag and handed it to Bocephus. He took the 9mm Glock for himself.

They hurried across the parking lot and pushed into the shop just as Naughty Betty reached for the door to throw the lock. Their momentum knocked her backward and she stumbled into a display of vibrators. The wire rack from which they hung caught her wig and pulled it half-off when she righted herself.

"Damn," Bocephus exclaimed, "she's a dude!"

Darrell blinked twice but said nothing as Naughty Betty removed her wig. He locked the door behind them and used the barrel of the Glock to direct her behind the cash register while he remained on the customer side of the counter. "Open it."

"Hey, Darrell, what's this?"

Exasperated, Darrell turned toward his younger brother. As he did, Naughty Betty grabbed the black leather punishment paddle kept beside the cash register and smashed it down on Darrell's wrist, causing him to swear as he released his grip on the Glock. "You broke my fucking wrist!"

Naughty Betty picked up the Glock.

Bocephus saw what happened, leveled his .32 at Naughty Betty, and pulled the trigger. The hammer clicked on an empty chamber. He pulled the trigger again and again with the same result each time. "Hey, Darrell, my gun ain't loaded. Why ain't my gun loaded?"

Before Darrell could answer, Bocephus threw the little revolver at Naughty Betty, but missed. The gun struck Darrell in the temple and clattered to the floor.

Naughty Betty pressed the barrel of the Glock against Darrell's other temple. Her voice, though still deep, was no longer sultry as when he first visited her shop. "Is your gun loaded, Darrell?"

Wide-eyed, he nodded.

"Then you won't give me any trouble, will you?"

Darrell shook his head.

Naughty Betty grabbed two pairs of plush love cuffs from the other side of the cash register and threw them toward Bocephus. As Bocephus caught one and the other clattered to the floor, she said, “Tell your friend—”

“Brother.”

“Even better.” Naughty Betty smiled. “Turn toward me. Lay face down on the counter and put your hands behind your back. Tell your brother to put one pair of the cuffs on you.”

“Darrell, I ain’t—”

“Do what he says!”

Bocephus stepped up behind his brother and fastened one pair of the plush love cuffs to his wrists.

“Now tell him to pick up the pair he dropped and put them on, behind his back.”

“But, Darrell—”

“Do it!”

Bocephus did as instructed.

After Naughty Betty made them get on their knees beside one another, she stepped behind them, checked to ensure that their cuffs were tight, and pulled off their stocking masks. She walked around in front and looked closely at Darrell. “You were in here the other day.”

“I was,” Darrell admitted.

“You were asking about special orders.”

Darrell nodded.

Bocephus interrupted, “What did you want to know about special orders for, Darrell? What was you going to order?”

Naughty Betty pointed the Glock at Bocephus but spoke to Darrell. “Can you shut him up before I do?”

“You going to call the cops?” Bocephus asked.

“Bo—Bocephus! Shut the fuck up!”

“But—”

Naughty Betty struck the side of Darrell’s head with the butt of the Glock, knocking him to the floor.

“What’d you do that for?” Bocephus demanded.

Naughty Betty placed the Glock on the counter, took a ball gag from a nearby shelf, and strapped it onto Bocephus, silencing him. Then she fit a full-face black lambskin hood — one with no openings except for the nose — over Bocephus’s head and laced it up the back.

When she finished with Bocephus, Naughty Betty jerked Darrell off the floor and onto his knees. She strapped a ball gag onto Darrell and covered his head with a second full-face black lambskin hood.

She took a moment to catch her breath before she picked up her cellphone and dialed the number for one of her clients, one who often placed special orders. When he answered, she said, “Clive, it’s Naughty Betty. Bring your van round back of the shop. I have a couple of new toys I think you’ll enjoy.”

All in a Day's Work

Pamela Kenney

Stan looked with irritation at the specks of blood on his brand new suit.

"Goddammit," he said, trying to brush the offending spots away. "I got this to go to funerals."

"You should always get black," Lenny said. "Hides the blood stains."

"Oh great. Now you're the fashion police."

"I'm just saying."

"Yeah well, just say something else."

"You could wear it to Frankie Testarossa's funeral. He won't be surprised."

Frankie weakly raised his head and glared at them with his one good eye.

"Hey, this isn't a joke," Stan said. "You know much it costs for dry cleaning?"

"Well that's because you can't take your suits just anywhere. You have to be selective. Which means they got you over a barrel."

"Ain't that the truth."

Stan sighed and wearily pointed his gun at Frankie, "So are we finished with this guy or what?"

"Yeah."

"Good," Stan said, taking aim at Frankie's forehead. "Do you want one or two, Frankie?"

"Fuck you," Frankie mumbled around his broken teeth.

"Very nice. For famous last words, those are pretty classy." Stan assumed the position and took aim.

Frankie closed his good eye and sighed deeply.

"Oh!" Lenny said, smacking his hand against his forehead.

Stan raised his eyes, and his gun to the ceiling. "What?"

"There was that thing."

"What thing?"

"That thing the boss wanted. Remember?"

"No."

"He said make sure we found out about…"

"About?"

"About…something. I can't remember. Don't you? It was really important."

"Are you fucking kidding me with this," Frankie asked from his corner of the room.

"Just be quiet over there," Stan said to Frankie while Lenny started rummaging around in his pockets.

"C'mon kill me already. What, I gotta wait all day over here?"

"You'll get your turn."

"This is so unprofessional." Frankie shook his head with disgust at the two mobsters.

"Unprofessional? I'll show you unprofessional," Stan yelled, striding over to Frankie and sticking the barrel of the gun against his head. "How's this for unprofessional?"

"Better. That's better. Now pull the trigger. What, I gotta do everything for you two losers?"

"Losers? Oh, now you did it!"

Just as Stan put his finger on the trigger, Lenny slapped a hand on his shoulder, stopping him.

"What," Stan asked savagely, turning to glare at Lenny, only there was a post-it note in the way.

"Am I supposed to be able to read what that says?"

Lenny moved the written side of the sticky note back in front of his own face and said, "The boss wrote it."

"Oh, great," Frankie muttered from his chair.

"Oh, I know," Lenny said, searching through another pocket.

"What now," Stan asked.

"I put a reminder on my phone. So, I wouldn't forget."

Stan and Frankie wearily watched as Lenny patted down yet more pockets. Pants pockets. Suit jacket pockets. The pockets of his overcoat.

"Take your time," Frankie muttered.

"It's here. Don't rush me," Lenny said, starting the circuit all over again, this time with a little more panic. "Where the hell did I put my phone?"

"Did you leave it in the fridge again," Stan asked.

Lenny just shook his head, but the tips of his ears started to turn red.

"Maybe you threw it out with your fast food again."

"Seriously?" Frankie looked at Stan with disbelief, attempting to raise an eyebrow.

Stan smiled at Frankie and nodded.

"Can you believe it? We're sifting through half eaten burgers and fries and crap. Of course, the fucking thing went right down to the bottom of the garbage can. That's the reason I had to get a new suit."

Lenny, who was completely red faced by this point, was standing next to a pile of his pocket contents. Bits of paper and post it notes, keys and chewing gum, Nicorette and cigarettes, a rabbit's foot and switchblade, brass knuckles and two guns.

"How often does this happen?" Frankie sighed.

"Fuck, you don't want to know." Stan lit up a cigarette and stuck it in Frankie's mouth.

"Manks," Frankie mumbled around the smoke.

Muttering started up across the room as Lenny became more and more agitated.

Before Stan could even say anything, Lenny started gibbering feverishly.

"It was really important Stan. The boss was crazy, remember. That vein was sticking out on his forehead. If we don't come back with it, he's going to kill us."

Stan vaguely remembered something, but the boss was losing it almost continuously these days, so it was impossible to tell when he was crazier than usual.

"Let's see the note again."

Lenny searched his pile of papers until he found the right one. After squinting at it for a few minutes, Stan said, "Thunder Mary?"

"The second word is money isn't it?"

"Tribank Money! Yeah, you're right. I do remember. He was really worked up about it. He said that money had never been found and it belonged to him."

"Right." Lenny beamed while Stan gave him a slap on the back.

"Good job, Lenny."

But their high was short lived because when they turned to look at Frankie, he was staring off into space, completely lifeless.

Like a corpse.

"Fuck!"

Stan and Lenny rushed to his side.

"Frankie?"

Silence.

"Oh Stan, what are we going to do?"

Lenny looked like he was about to cry when Stan held up a hand and pointed to the end of the cigarette, where a very small cloud of smoke formed and gently blew away.

“Frankie, do you know anything about the Tribank money?”

Silence reigned as Frankie continued to stare, dead eyed, at the opposite wall.

Then another puff of smoke.

“Don’t make me jab you in the bullet hole.”

Frankie’s good eye rolled toward Stan with unbridled hatred. Drawing in a ragged breath through his broken nose and puffing it out sharply through his mouth, Frankie ejected the cigarette.

“What?”

“Tribank money?”

“Yeah.”

“You know where it is?”

Silence.

“Cig.”

“What?”

“Cig!”

“Oh.” Stan picked the still smoking cigarette off the floor and held it to Frankie’s mouth long enough for one drag before removing it again. “Well?”

“Yeah. I know,” Frankie said, reluctantly.

“Okay, we’re going for a ride. You’re going to give us directions,” Stan said, as he reinserted the cigarette into Frankie’s mouth.

It only took forty-five minutes and one detour when Stan thought Frankie said right when he meant left until they reached a desolate place in the woods. The city lights created a glow off to the east but all around them was densely wooded forest and one track just big enough for the car that soon petered out into nothing a little further from where they parked.

"Okay where?"

Frankie pointed and looking out the window, the boys could see a mound of turned earth.

"C'mon Lenny."

"What about him?"

"Oh yeah. Prop him against that tree. He'll be out of the way over there. I'll get the shovels."

"Hey, this way we only have to dig once. We can put Frankie in when we're done. How does that sound Frankie?"

Lenny turned in his seat, smiling warmly at Frankie.

"Fuck you, asshole."

"Geez, you're touchy aren't ya?"

"Stop dicking around Lenny. Let's get this done," Stan said, taking off his suit jacket and laying it out with care on the front seat of the car.

About half an hour later, from his front row seat, Frankie saw the explosion. The blast sent both Stan and Lenny soaring quite a distance and when they finally hit the ground, they didn't move again. Ever.

Chunks off both of them landed near Frankie but most sailed closer to the car.

"Thanks guys," Frankie muttered, waiting for the dust to settle before he started crawling to the gaping hole left in the earth, picking up a shoe clad foot en route and tossing it over his shoulder.

Frankie wondered how he was going to get to the money, what with Bill having rigged up the booby trap and Joe in possession of the trigger that deactivated the bomb. It was the plan the three of them had devised to create a feeling of mutual trust and understanding.

Of course, that plan didn't work out too well when Bill got himself arrested, which caused Joe to take off for parts unknown.

But things have a funny way of working themselves out, thought Frankie, as he peered over the edge of the crater at the exposed lock box, gleaming in the moonlight.

Thick as Thieves

Chris R. Young

In the middle of the night one Hallowe'en, Fingers Malloy and Barney Felchett crept along the back alley between the tall, murky London tenements. High above them, laundry flapped in a gentle breeze, and clouds passed intermittently over a full, bright moon that seemed to scrutinize their every move. A small dark figure, disturbed from its foraging in a dust-can, leapt from the lid with a squeal and knocked over an empty glass bottle that skittered along the alley floor.

Fingers and Barney froze.

"What was that?" whispered Barney, the younger of the two.

"Just a cat," Fingers said.

"What?"

"It was just a cat, I said." He made to go on, but Barney placed his hand on Fingers' shoulder.

"A cat?" he said, his eyes wide and frightened – two white orbs high up and close together in a black stubbly face crowned with shoulder length greasy locks. "Was it a black cat? You don't think – you know – it being Hallowe'en?"

Fingers stared at him. "Don't be ridiculous," he said, and looked round at the darkened windows, rubbing his goatee. "Now which one is it?"

But Barney hadn't moved. He could have been made of plaster of Paris. "I 'eard 'the Nutcracker' spent a bit of time with witch doctors in the Congo,"

"Witch doctors?" said Fingers, who was in his fifties, of slight build, and approaching normal retirement age for the profession.

"The dangerous ones," said Barney quietly, eyes scanning the gloom. "They say 'e learned to cast curses on people 'e don't like."

"Bollocks," Fingers grunted. "Frank 'The Nutcracker' Groyle hasn't been further'n Milton Keynes. Probably started them rumours 'imself just to give people the willies." He sniffed, patted Barney on the cheek and pushed him along the alley.

On they crept through the narrow back-street, dried leaves crunching underfoot, skirting around garbage and crouching beneath windowsills. A woman's scream from some classic horror film drifted down through an open balcony window several stories up and made Barney flinch.

"Why do we have to rob the Nutcracker's bookies anyway?" Barney whispered, suppressing a shiver and training the pen-light back on the map. "There's a lot easier jobs we could do."

"I already told you," Fingers murmured. "Because the Grand National was this afternoon, odds are Frank's safe will be bursting with takings until the banks open on Monday."

"Who'd you bet on?"

Fingers gave an exasperated shake of his head. "Some damn three-legged nag."

"She win?"

Fingers stared. "No."

"No wonder, with a name like that."

The two men studied each other in silence.

"Look, gimme the map," Fingers said at last, reaching for it.

"Get off it, Fingers," said Barney, drawing back. "I said I can do it, and I will."

"I just don't want any slip ups, that's all." Fingers' beard bristled in the moonlight. "Not tonight."

Barney turned back and tapped the penlight on Fingers' chest. "You know what your trouble is, Fingers? You got no faith in people."

A flicker of hurt touched the older man's face. He recalled a time when his son had said almost the same thing. A time many years ago, when they had still talked.

"All right," he nodded at last. "Let's get on with it."

The two men pushed on, Fingers glancing behind them every so often, his bag of tools clanking against his hip, as Barney looked at the map from different angles and counted the narrow gaps between buildings leading to the high street.

After a while Barney stopped and said, "This is it."

"You sure?"

"Positive," whispered Barney. "Now hold me bag while I go an' attend to business."

Fingers did so and tried to peer into one of the windows while holding up his free hand to block out his own reflection. He could see a desk in the murk, and perhaps a sink, but not much else.

A grunt of effort followed by a breath of relief came from Barney's direction.

Fingers rolled his eyes in the darkness. "Barney, come on. Every single time."

"Can't 'elp it," Barney muttered over his shoulder. "It's the excitement."

A foul odour that could have emanated from the very depths of Hell itself casually drifted down the alley.

"'Eaven's sake, Barney," Fingers crossed himself and looked pleadingly up at the sky. "You could at least have gone downwind."

Barney came back with a faint smile of contentment on his face. "Right then, let's get started."

With an exasperated grunt, Fingers put the penlight in his mouth and examined the window frame. He followed the wires until he came to two sensors straddling the gap between frame and window. He removed his wallet, opened a flap, and took out a razor blade pre-prepared with a strip of double-sided tape. He peeled off the layer of plastic and let it flutter away, turning his attention back to the sensors. Holding his breath, and very, very slowly, he slipped the razor blade between the two white plastic cuboids.

No alarm sounded.

He continued until it was all the way in, every second prepared for the howl of a klaxon smashing the silence to smithereens. But at last the blade was positioned correctly and he pressed it to the wooden frame with the tape to hold it in place.

Fingers let out his breath. Looked like they'd gotten over the first hurdle. But suddenly he was sure Barney was in the process of swinging something heavy at the glass. He spun around to see Barney standing quietly watching.

"Finished?" Barney said.

Fingers took a deep breath and let it out slow. "Yes," he murmured. Just jittery, he thought. "Yes, all set."

"Let's get it bleedin' done then."

"Actually," Fingers mumbled, stroking his beard, "I'm a little surprised at how basic his security is. Perhaps there's some other form of entry detection device we don't know about. Floor sensors. Infrared beams. Things like that."

Barney eyes moved from the window frame, to Fingers' face and back again.

"Well," shrugged Fingers. "We'll see." He removed a long narrow sliver of metal from inside his coat and worked it in between the window and frame at the latch. With a twist, he had it open. Then he crouched down and picked up a handful of gravel from the alley floor.

"You gonna chuck that in there?" Barney asked.

"Better we know about the sensors out here than in there."

Barney shrugged.

They both peered into the gloom.

"Get ready," said Fingers. After a deep breath, he tossed the handful of gravel into the darkness.

The two men got ready to bolt.

But the only sound was of the gravel bouncing off the floor inside.

They looked at each other. "So far so good," said Fingers.

"Famous last words."

"Masks on. Probably cameras inside."

Fingers pulled his ski-mask over his head, held the penlight between his teeth and eased a leg, his head and his arm through the window. Once fully inside, he swept the room with the light to reveal some kind of kitchenette area, with a door leading off to what was probably the main office next to the sink. It was open, with darkness beyond. A kettle, dirty cups, a sugar bowl and some teaspoons lay on the table nearby, while a small fridge hummed quietly in the corner.

Fingers' senses were one hundred percent alert. He could hear and smell Barney follow him in through the window behind him. Every fibre of his being was strained to its limit as adrenalin did its stuff. Careful not to let the metal surface of the penlight touch his fillings, he angled his head slightly to throw the light's reach beyond the doorway into the other room.

"What's wrong with the light?" came Barney's hoarse voice.

"Nothing," said Fingers, without turning round. "It's working fine. What do you mean?"

Barney gasped suddenly. "You mean it's on?" There was a rustling sound.

"Course it's on," said Fingers, gritted teeth still clamped around the penlight. He could almost see through the doorway. His heart took a sudden leap in his chest as the shard of light revealed what seemed to be the edge and top corner of that which he loved and lived for most.

A very large safe.

"Oh my God!" Barney suddenly shouted from behind him, causing Fingers to jump into the air, the hairs of his beard standing on end. "I can’t see! My eyes, he’s cursed my eyes!"

Fingers spun round, shining the light directly onto Barney's face.

And recoiled with an involuntary spasm.

What stood before Fingers was not Barney as he knew him, but a hideous apparition that burned its image forever onto his mind. Greasy black seaweed squirmed from Barney's eye-sockets, rippling and shifting over itself! The stuff was vomiting from his nose and mouth in long, hideous rivulets, reaching out for him like the tentacles of a deadly poisonous sea creature!

"*Jesus!*" Fingers shouted, the penlight falling from his mouth and hitting the floor with a clatter, leaving them in darkness. Fingers tried to scream, but he couldn't. No sound came. He bit instead on his fist and crouched down with his back to the fridge, whimpering.

"I'm blind!" Barney shrieked in a muffled voice around the black oily tentacles. Or as if ... Fingers stopped whimpering and removed his fist from his mouth.

As if he was talking through fabric.

Fingers took a deep breath and let it out slowly. Then he reached around for the torch, found it, and gave it a twist, but the light wouldn't come on. The bulb had shattered.

"My eyes! I'm cursed!"

"Oh, shut up, Barney," Fingers muttered as he clambered to his feet in the darkness. "For God's sake." He grabbed Barney by the shoulders and spun him round. "You've just got your ski-mask on backwards."

"I -" stuttered Barney, "I do?"

"Ye-es."

There was the sound of cloth moving over greasy hair, followed by the noise of a middle-aged burglar suddenly comprehending. Barney cleared his throat. "Could happen to anyone," he said.

"Indeed," replied Fingers. "Should probably have instructions printed on the label." He rolled his eyes in disbelief. *Jesus, Mary and Joseph,* he thought. *What have I let myself in for?*

"I've got a bad feeling about this one," said Barney, his ski-mask now on the right way round. "First the cat, then the suspiciously light security, next my ski-mask, and now the pen-light's busted." There was the sound of nervous scratching. "And it's quiet...too quiet."

"Barney," groaned Fingers, chewing on the section of beard beneath his lower lip. "All of those are either nothing, good things, or your fault."

"My fault? You're the one broke the light! And if I'm not mistaken, you're the one what wanted to break into the Nutcracker's bookies, not me! I'm pretty sure I was against it right from the start!"

"All right, be quiet, will you? Look, we're in now. Yes, the pen-light's busted, but it's a full moon and we can still see a little by the moonlight. And they don't call me 'Fingers' for nothing."

"Is it because," Barney muttered, "you're a butter-fingers?"

Fingers' beard bristled through his mask. He turned away from his partner towards the doorway leading to the office.

"Or is it because you eat a lot of," Barney's mind was obviously in top gear, "fish-fingers?"

Fingers crept towards the doorway, his hands splayed out in front of him.

"Or, wait," said Barney, pointing at the ceiling. "P'raps it's because you like to smell your fingers. You know, after..."

Fingers spun round and bunched Barney's lapels in his fists so fast Barney had no idea what was going on. He pulled him so close their noses touched. "Barney, shut up or I swear to God, I will ram your head into that little fridge down there and leave you for the Nutcracker to 'ave 'is evil way with."

Barney was silent. The only sound was of Fingers' heavy breathing. And the humming of the fridge, suddenly shivering to a halt as if it knew it was being threatened.

"All right, all right," said Barney. "I went over the line. I apologize. Now let's just get the job done and get out of here, eh?"

Fingers held the grip a second longer and then released his - he had just decided - soon-to-be-ex partner.

He turned back to the safe in the other room, barely visible in the moonlight, and crouched down in front. It looked like a standard X76 OP1 Mach 3 Mega Chunk Titanium three-lock safe, in metallic grey, with rounded corners and no doubt a red velvet interior.

Behind him, Fingers heard Barney flatten his ruffled jacket with a mildly offended air and shuffle around the gloom.

"Don't touch anything," said Fingers, without glancing up. "And keep quiet. Do you think you can manage that?"

"I don't take orders from you," said Barney.

"Oh yes you do," said Fingers, removing his gloves and cracking his knuckles. "If you want any of what's inside this safe, you do."

Barney snorted.

Leaving prints was not very good. But Fingers believed cracking a safe was like taking off a woman's bra. And vice versa. Best done au naturel. He needed to feel the surface of the safe beneath his skin, to understand every contour, every grain in the steel, especially in the dark.

He welcomed the old familiar glow in the pit of his stomach, the warmth in his hands, the flutter in his heart. Then he leant his head forward and went to work.

"Opening safes isn't that hard, you know," Barney said *sotto voce* in the darkness.

Fingers ignored him. He loved the sound of the dial as it clicked around its casing. A sweeter symphony was never heard. The safe spoke to him, singing, telling him all her secrets.

In another world outside this rapture, Fingers could hear Barney mumbling to himself. The sound of something falling to the floor. A thud, followed by "Ouch." But none of it mattered. Fingers was encompassed in a bubble of light all of his own - a mythical golden cloud often discussed, but rarely experienced, in the sacred Buddhist shrines in the mountains of Tibet.

Suddenly there was a click as the last of the tumblers dropped into place. Something inside Fingers blossomed and he closed his eyes and touched his forehead to the door of the safe. Then he pulled on his gloves, wiped down the dial, and laid a hand on the heavy handle.

"We in?" Barney called from the room's murky depths.

"Sure are," murmured Fingers with a hairy grin, and put his hand on the handle. "Prepare to see a very large amount of cash indeed." With that, he pushed down and heaved.

The safe door swung open with a faint squeak.

Empty!

He felt right to the back and all around inside the safe, but apart from the velvet interior, the only thing inside was air.

"What?" said Fingers, "No, it can't be. I don't understand."

Barney stepped over. "What is it?"

"It's empty."

"Oh, great," said Barney. "That's just vunderbar, Fingers."

He scratched at his head. "I don't get it. It should be bursting with cash."

"Guess you're not so smart after all, eh Fingers?" Barney chuckled. "Perhaps you should change your name to Thumbs."

"Unless..." Fingers was thinking again. "... there's a back-up safe, hidden somewhere. And this one's just for petty cash."

"What makes you think there's another safe in here, Thumbs?"

"Call it instinct, Barney. Intuition. Knowing the unknowable."

Barney made a reference to his own genitalia.

"Come on," Fingers murmured. "Let's look around. It'll probably be behind a picture or set in the floor or something."

The two of them explored the room, looking for another safe.

Suddenly there was a chuckle.

"What's so funny?" said Fingers.

"What?" said Barney.

"What you laughing at?"

"I didn't laugh," said Barney. "Your hearing-aid's on the blink, Thumbs."

Son of a bitch, thought Fingers. *I'll get him for this. If he wasn't my wife's brother, I'd ...*

They resumed their search. Fingers looked under a rug, in bookshelves, behind paintings, and anywhere else he could think of. But the near darkness made it tough going.

At last Barney called out from the other side of the room, "Found it!"

"Shh!" said Fingers, hurrying over. "Not so loud. Where is it?"

"Right in the wall here. Just as you said." Barney placed Fingers' hands on what felt like a picture frame on a hinge, behind which, set into the wall, was none other than a model JAX 5000 Smithsonite Invisi-Safe Type Gama, with vacuum-sealed door and fireproof surface.

"Well, I'll be," whispered Fingers with some admiration. "This is top of the range. The man spares no expense when it comes to security. Even a direct hit with a five-megaton nuclear missile wouldn't destroy this beauty."

"You mean you can't open it?"

Fingers chuckled. "Oh, I can open it, all right." He clicked his knuckles and blew on the tips of his fingers. "You mark my words, Barney."

As Fingers searched in his tool bag for some equipment, he heard a rustling coming from Barney's direction.

"What are you doing?"

"Taking me ski-mask off. Me ‘ead's too hot, and I'm sweating like a flamingo's armpits in this get up. Besides. I reckon any cameras won't be able to see our mugs clearly in the dark."

"Hmm," said Fingers, his hands paused mid rummage. "Good point." He pulled off his own mask and thrust it in his tool bag.

At last he found it - an electronic device with two electro-magnets on sticky pads. This safe was the keypad type, with a 6-digit entry code. Meant the password would be one in several billion permutations. Much easier to circumnavigate the electronics and just override the signals controlling the locks using electro-magnets.

"Opening safes is easy. Anyone with the right gadgetry can do it," Barney opined from his position in the dark. "The hard part is locating the safe in the first place." He was leaning against a desk-like object with his arms folded.

Fingers paid him no attention. He removed the plastic from the sticky surfaces of the magnetic pads and affixed one on either side of the keypad, securing them firmly to the safe's surface. Then he switched on the device, read the backlit screen that cast an eerie glow on his bearded jowls, and adjusted the controls. It wasn't just about having the right equipment, he knew. Even after you've attached the pads in the right places, working the gain too high or low could overload the magnets and set off an anti-tamper alarm inside the safe.

A faint snoring sound came from Barney.

Fingers concentrated on the red and blue LEDs on the device's display, until finally ...

Buzz. Whirr. Click.

"Bingo," Fingers said under his breath.

The safe door unlocked and swung slowly open on well-oiled hinges.

"Whassut?" said Barney.

"It's payday, Barnes." He reached his arm into the black space, fingers stretched out to grab the bales of cash that ... were not ... actually there. His hand felt nothing but the upper and lower metal grills.

"No," Fingers hissed. "No, no, no, *Damn* it!"

"What is it this time?" Barney murmured groggily. "Don't tell me -"

"Nothing there."

"Not possible."

"I don't believe this." Fingers ran his fingers through his hair, leaving it sticking up in alarming tufts. "It doesn't make any sense. I mean even if there was no money, there still should be documents, insurance policies, brown envelopes or something inside."

"Containing photos of important people in compromising positions, you mean?"

"For example, yes."

"And both safes were empty?"

"Completely."

"You're sure."

"Absolutely."

"No hidden compartments?"

"Unlikely."

"You know," said Barney, "Sherlock Holmes once said that after you eliminate all other possibilities, the only remaining possibility, no matter how improbable, must be the truth."

"And what is that remaining possibility?"

"We're not very good at this."

"Now that is improbable. I don't want to blow my own trumpet, but I've been opening safes since before you were potty-trained, Barney m'lad. I've worked with the best of 'em. Slasher McFee and I did that bank job together back in '68. Donald Allibaster and I pulled off the famous jewellery store burglary of '74. I'm proud to say that I was there when Willy Macanally and his band of merry burglars broke into the Customs and Excise holding house in '87 and liberated several tonnes of duty free. None of these crimes have been solved, Barney old son. None of them. They were perfect each and every one, and all of those legendary men are now where they belong, on the beaches of Ibiza, Bermuda, and Torre Melenos respectively, because they're not criminals Barney, they're artists, *artists,* and they are reaping what they have sowed. The good life."

"All right, all right. 'Blimey Fingers, that's the most I've ever 'eard you say in one breath."

"Just stop going on about how easy it is to open safes, all right?"

"I'm not going on about it."

"You were."

"I wasn't," said Barney.

The two men looked roughly in each other's direction as Fingers tried to recover his breath.

"Look," said Barney, "let's just get out of here and go 'ome, all right? I'll buy us a vindaloo."

Fingers pulled the device crudely from the safe door and dumped it unceremoniously in his tool bag. "All right," he said quietly. He picked up his bag and the two men made their way back the way they had come.

There would be other days. Other triumphs.

Fingers was almost at the door to the kitchenette when he heard Barney curse.

"What is it, now?" he said.

"I don't believe it."

"What," Fingers said, turning round.

"I think I've just found another safe."

Fingers' ears pricked up. He walked over to where he could see Barney's outline. "I hit me ankle off it earlier," Barney said. "Thought it was just a small filing cabinet. But it's got one of them dials on the front."

"Hmm," said Fingers, crouching down. It was a mini Triple X Trojan 500. "This one's unlikely to have anything in it if the JAX 5000 was empty. But still, as we're here. Never look a gift horse in the mouth," Fingers began removing his gloves again. "Not even a Trojan one." He paused, as an idea blossomed in the darkness.

"What is it?" said Barney.

"Well, it's just what you were saying earlier."

"What was that?"

"About how opening safes wasn't all that difficult. That anyone could do it."

"Mm hmm..."

"Why don't you have a crack at this one, Barney? The Triple X Trojan 500 isn't so tricky. Why not give her a whirl, see how she handles?"

"Er, you know, I don't think -"

"Oh, come on, Barney? Don't be shy."

"Well...it can't be that difficult," Barney said, crouching down and taking off his gloves.

"That's the spirit," chuckled Fingers. He'll never get this open in a million years.

"Right then," muttered Barney, putting his ear to the safe door. "A twiddle to the left ... a twiddle to the right ..."

Twiddle all you like, Fingers grinned to himself. Teach you to mock me you ... you amateur.

"Listen for the click ..." said Barney quietly, " ... aaand, there you have it." He pressed down on the handle, which gave with a *thunk*, and the door swung smoothly open.

Fingers' jaw almost hit the floor, crashed through it into the basement and hit the floor of that too.

"What did I tell you? Nothing to it." Fingers could see Barney's huge smile reflecting in the moonlight like a Cheshire cat. "Don't know why you go on like it's some big thing all the time."

Fingers was stunned to his veteran safe-cracker core. "How ... You ... What ..." He opened and closed his mouth like a stranded fish. At last he managed, "Well, is there anything inside?"

"Ah hah, well, if you want any of what's in this safe, you'll have to take some orders from me from now on, Fingers, *me old son*," Barney said, crouching down and reaching his hand inside.

Just as he did so, all the lights went on.

Fingers, immediately blinded, could discern nothing at all behind the sudden glare on his wide-open pupils. "What the -" he said.

"Woah," cried Barney, trying to cover his eyes with the back of his hand.

"Party's over, gentlemen," said a strange new voice. "If you'd be good enough to place any weapons you may have on the floor and step over here with your hands in the air, we would be most grateful."

As the blindness dissipated, Fingers could make out a large group of policemen standing near the front door, and that the room they were in was filled with several silvery cuboid shapes.

"I'm blind," Barney whimpered.

"You have the right to remain silent," said the strange new voice. "Anything you do say, can and will be taken down and used in evidence against you. You have the right to a lawyer. If you cannot afford a lawyer ..."

"Damn," said Fingers, throwing his hands up in exasperation. "We've been rumbled. What was it, the alarm in the JAX 5000?"

"No," said the voice, belonging to a tall, mustachioed detective inspector, emerging from the glare.

"The window?"

"Not even that," said the D.I.

"Then how?"

"Mr. Jones in the tenement round the back heard a cat knock a bottle over, looked out his window ready to throw a boot, and saw you two unsavoury characters creepin' about. Being a good law-abiding citizen, he made the right choice and called us."

Fingers, his eyesight finally clearing, saw that a couple of policemen wore night vision goggles, and another had a long-distance microphone. A sinking feeling opened up in his stomach.

"We've been standing out there for the past thirty minutes enjoying the show," continued the copper, "waiting to see exactly what you were up to."

That's when Fingers realized they were not in a bookies. The silver cuboids in the large room, to his great chagrin, were all safes. About thirty of them. Some open, some closed, all of them brand sparkling new.

Fingers and Barney looked at each other.

"We thought you were going to do the bookies next door," continued the D.I.

A couple of policemen chuckled.

"But we certainly appreciate your generously supplied information about Slasher McFee, Donald Allibaster and Willy Macanally. That was very civil of you." The detective inspector said to one of his men, "Get on the blower will you, Sergeant?"

"Right away, sir," the man said and strode off. The D.I. turned back to the two burglars. "Although it's still beyond our comprehension," he said, fighting back a grin, "why on Earth you'd want to break into Mr. Jones' safe shop."

Hic

Tom Barlow

Grand theft auto is the first crime that Gloria, the woman with whom he is probably in love, springs on Andy Garver this Friday evening. He's been dating his brother's ex-lover for a couple of weeks and he is still afraid that the slightest discord will kill the fragile relationship, so he doesn't bail immediately. Gloria has shown up at his door in an F-150 pickup that he's never seen before. It belongs, she explains as she pulls away from the curb, to a guy that she dated two years previous. He uses a company car for his evening gig delivering pizzas, so if they get the truck back before midnight, he'll never know it has been gone.

"You hot-wired it?" he says.

"No need," Gloria says. "I always copy the car keys of guys I date."

Andy makes a note to be careful with his car keys. "But why would you steal a truck?"

"You and I are going to have an adventure tonight."

He certainly doesn't like the sound of that. Gloria, lovely as she is, has a checkered past with a couple of arrests, although no convictions; one for dealing a little speed, one for playing on the affections of an elderly neighbor who wrote her check after check in the futile hope of bedding her.

Andy has never been brave enough to break the law, unlike his brother Clete, who is imprisoned for the next five to seven years for trying to cook meth in the back of his van.

"What kind of adventure?" he says, unable to keep worry out of his voice.

She takes the U.S. 23 exit south toward the Ohio River. "You know Butch Dean?"

"The drug dealer?" He knows about Dean. Anyone who grew up on the south side of Columbus knows him as a man with whom you do not fuck.

"Well, he fronted me ten grand a couple of weeks ago. I had a deal set up to buy some coke and turn it around for twice what I paid. It was a one time-thing, a slam dunk." She is ignoring the speed limit, as usual, even though they are in a stolen vehicle.

Andy isn't surprised that Gloria is mixed up in dope, since she'd run with his brother, but he is surprised she is in at that level. "Didn't work out?"

"Cash is a bad thing to have in your hands when you live in a town with a casino and you have a gambling problem."

"You lost the money before you could buy the dope?"

"Bingo." She cuts off a school bus coasting toward a red light. "His people have been looking for me for the last week; I'm lucky that very few people know where I live."

"So how are you going to get the money to pay him back?" He has longed to share intimacies with Gloria, but the reality isn't living up to his expectations.

"That's where you come in." She reaches over, placing a hand on his thigh. "I need your help to hold up a Boosters Club. Clete always says you know how to keep your mouth shut, so I figure you and me are a perfect team." She gives him a devilish grin, but there is a steely resolve in her big blues.

"You want me to help you with a robbery?" Andy takes a quick inventory of his life to date. A crappy job hustling car parts from the warehouse to auto garages. A shitty room in a boarding house, the rest of his income going to pay for smokes and rent for a mother who barely deserves the title. Compare that to the chance to have a dynamite girlfriend and a wad of cash. He knows what Clete would choose, has always chosen. And he is the smarter brother.

"You're full of questions this evening," she says. "But yeah, I want your help. Your size will scare the shit out of them, and I've got a gun. Between the two of us we shouldn't have any trouble. And you could go home with a few grand or so for the effort."

He stares at Gloria's profile. He'd run into her dozens of times in the three years since Clete went to prison, and she hadn't even bothered to nod to him. Then one night two weeks earlier she walked into the McDonald's while he was eating his McRib and suddenly, she was asking if she could join him, she was talking a mile a minute about the job she'd just lost at K-Mart, as though they were old friends. They've spent every evening since together. Now he wonders if she has just been cruising for a partner in crime.

Still he can't help but marvel at her beauty: untamed tightly curled black hair flowing off her shoulders like a wind scoop, a sharp jaw line that tapers to a fetching cleft chin, plump lips just made to carry the scarlet lipstick she favors, eyes the color of glacial melt, and knockers that he fantasizes burying himself between.

He isn't a bad looking guy himself, according to his grandma. She sees a bit of Bogart in his face, especially when his five o'clock shadow arrives. Most women, however, are put off by his size, six feet six with the build of a linebacker, size that belies his timid nature.

"It's just this one time, right?" he finally says.

"Just this once, I promise," she says, and slides her hand over slightly.

They arrive at the stadium while there is still fifteen minutes on the scoreboard clock. The host school, Piers

High, is ahead, and a pleased buzz is coming from the packed stadium.

Gloria parks at the far end of the huge parking lot, beyond the coverage of the security cameras. They are almost invisible in the November dark made deeper by overhanging maple branches. As they wait for the game to end, she explains the heist. The volunteers who run the Boosters' concessions will be busy in the school counting the evening take, which she hopes will be between $15,000 and $20,000. All cash; they don't take credit cards. She plans to intercept the person in charge of the deposit on his way to his car.

As Gloria explains her plans, Andy's legs begin to twitch, and he presses down on his knees to still them.

"You nervous?"

"Yeah," Andy says.

"I need you cool, OK?" she says, eyes locked on his.

He's too nervous hold her gaze, fixes on the stadium lights.

After a moment she nods, although he has made no response. "OK, we have time. Let's get you calmed down." She leans over and unzips his jeans, reaches within and withdraws his immediately hard penis. He watches in blissful amazement as she briskly jacks him off.

After he comes, he zips up, slumps down in his seat, even more deeply in love.

"Better?" she says, chuckling softly.

"Oh my God."

"Glad I could help."

He wonders if he is expected to return the favor. "You nervous?"

She rolls her eyes. "No, thanks."

A few minutes later the crowd begins streaming out of the stadium to the sound of the band playing the school fight song. Once the crowd has totally dispersed and the stadium lights go off, Gloria leads him across the dark blacktop toward the school.

When they reach the building, they step behind a couple of the head-high arborvitae lining the sidewalk from the school to the parking lot. Gloria takes her hand out of her pocket and squeezes his. "You cool now?" she whispers.

"Yeah," Andy says, although doubt and fear are beginning to override his carnal afterglow.

She hands him a ski mask and puts one on herself. He dons his and stands quietly beside her, wishing that he had taken a piss before he left the house.

They wait in the dark for an agonizing hour. Andy fights his tendency to hyperventilate when nervous.

Finally, the school doors open. Peering through the branches, Andy watches their prey approach, two of them: a short, plump woman in her 30s wearing a down coat that drags on the ground, and a man in his 50s in a chambray shirt that fails to completely contain his enormous gut.

Gloria grabs his sleeve and drags him behind her as she steps out onto the sidewalk in front of the two. The school security lights reflect from the barrel of the 9mm pistol she pulls from her jacket pocket. Andy takes his place beside her, blocking the couple's progress.

The two stop in their tracks, the woman gasping. Andy watches the man weigh his chances against the gun and Andy. He can read in the slump of the man's shoulders his conclusion he has nothing to gain by trying to play the hero.

"We'll take the money," Gloria says, waving the gun back and forth between the two.

"You can't take this. It's for the children," the woman says.

"It'll go to a good cause," Gloria says, reaching out for the woman's handbag and pulling it free.

The woman begins to cry. She reminds Andy of his aunt Tricia, gone for several years now, who broke down every time the children's choir sang at their church. Although Gloria has expressly forbidden him to talk, he wants to assure the woman that she is in no danger. However, he is more afraid of Gloria, and so keeps his lips zipped.

Except he hiccups.

They all looked at him. He hiccups again.

"At least give me my purse," the woman says, turning her attention back to Gloria. "It's of no use to you."

Gloria takes out the deposit bag, hands it to Andy, and lets the purse fall to the ground. Andy hiccups.

The woman nods a thanks her face doesn't reflect.

"Let's go," Gloria says. Andy hiccups as he follows her at a trot back to their truck. Every ten seconds or so he hiccups again.

Gloria doesn't turn on the lights of the truck until they are well clear of the school, so the people they've robbed won't be able to identify their vehicle.

They exchange the truck for Gloria's car without a hitch. Andy isn't sure what happens next; although he and Gloria have been hanging out together, they haven't reached the point where she's invited him home, and since he rents a room in a boarding house, he really has no discreet place to bring her.

This night, however, she drives him to her place without comment. "Help yourself to a beer," she says as she guides him into her apartment, a tiny one-bedroom in an apartment building that has the charm of an absentee landlord squeezing the last nickel out of his property. "Maybe that'll stop your hiccups."

He continues to hiccup every ten to fifteen seconds, though. After the first hour, it has grown quite annoying.

Andy notes that Gloria isn't much of a housekeeper. The coffee table is piled high with unopened packages of socks, stacks of DVDs, a dozen workout suits with the tags still attached, a new-in-the-package Xbox and bras and panties in a laundry basket. On the floor against the far wall sit two flat-screen televisions side by side.

Gloria takes a seat at the kitchen table. She opens the deposit bag and carefully unloads the cash, which has been separated into bundles of singles, fives, tens, twenties and a couple of hundreds.

Andy sits across from her and picks up a stack of twenties, fanning them for the pleasure of the ripple.

"Don't play with it," Gloria says. "Count."

It takes them fifteen minutes and forty-five hiccups to confirm what the deposit slip reads. $11,543.

Gloria sits back, smiling with satisfaction. "Not bad." She counts out $1,500 and hands it to Andy.

He has been so nervous about taking part in the actual holdup that he hasn't taken the time to dwell on the cash that is to come his way. As he fingers his new fortune, he wonders for the first time about fairness. Why not a 50/50 split?

Gloria, as though reading his mind, says, "I did all the planning, so I get the bigger share. After all, all you did was stand there."

He is intimidated by her now after seeing how deftly she handled that gun. He is also hopeful that he will be invited to spend the night, so he decides to live with her decision.

Their heist is, to her delight, the lead story on Channel 10's late Friday night news. The reporter, standing in front of Piers High, refers to the crime as the hiccup holdup, a joke that doesn't strike Andy as the least bit amusing. His hiccups grow worse as they watch the coverage.

He is glad that they live in Columbus, over 50 miles from Piers, so that even with his size he won't immediately come under suspicion as a potential culprit. If he can just shake the damned hiccups.

Whatever second thoughts about the situation he has dissolve that night when Gloria invites him into her bed.

He doesn't stay there long, though. Making love with her is better than he'd even imagined, but his continued hiccups have her sending him to sleep on the couch afterward. Since his car is ten miles away at his boarding house, he has no choice but to spend the night on the dilapidated futon.

He is awake all night, though, hiccupping and replaying the crime.

The first thing Gloria does on awaking the next morning is step out into the hallway and swipe her neighbor's *Columbus Dispatch.* Their robbery makes the front page, this time tagged as the hiccup heist. The paper estimates one of the assailants at six foot five or better.

As they eat their cereal, the milk on the verge of spoiling, Andy asks when she's going to give Dean his money.

"I'll catch him at the casino tomorrow night," she says. "He takes weekends off to spend with the family. I don't want to hand the dough to one of his goons, because I can't be sure it will get to him.

"In the meantime, your hiccups have got to go. Big as you are, anybody you talk to is going to make the connection. And I don't want you hanging around here forever, either. It's best if we aren't seen together for a while."

Andy is unclear if she is blowing him off or not, and doesn't want to pose the question for fear of receiving the answer he doesn't want. "I don't have anywhere to go," he says. "Hic. If I go back to the boarding house, they're going to expect me at every meal--I never miss one when I'm there--and when I stay in my room, they'll be suspicious."

"Then we'll have to get rid of your hiccups."

"How?" he says.

"Well," she says, "how about..." She suddenly screams and lunges across the table at him with her table knife.

He falls out of his chair as he evades her attack.

She leans over until she can see him on the floor. "Did that work?"

"Hic," he says.

"Damn."

They spend the morning trolling the internet for cures. Andy tries holding his breath in a variety of body contortions. He drinks glass after glass of water upright, upside down, sideways. He stands on his right leg, puts his left thumb in his left ear, and takes a drink of water. He has Gloria press lightly on his closed eyes as he takes a drink. He drinks a glass of water while holding a pencil clenched in his teeth. He has her pinch his nose shut while he drinks.

He takes a tablespoon full of brown sugar and dissolves it on his tongue. He bites into a lemon wedge drenched in hot sauce. He swallows air until he burps. He downs a teaspoon of peanut butter without chewing.

"Hic."

Gloria even ducks out for a quick run to the convenience store, returning with a couple of helium balloons. He cuts a small hole in one, breathes in the gas. All it does is raise his hiccups a couple of pitches.

"How long can this possibly go on?" he asks.

Gloria, reading up on the topic on her laptop, says, "Apparently, for years."

"Well, damn. Hic."

Early that afternoon, Andy turns on a golf tournament and, despite the hiccups, immediately falls asleep.

He awakes as Gloria returns around 4 p.m. with a bucket of fried chicken and a bottle of pills.

"What's that?" Andy says, pointing to the bottle.

"It's what doctors prescribe for hiccups," Gloria says. "Thorazine. It's usually a med for schizophrenia, but it works on the hiccups too. I gave a grand of your money to this girl I know works in a psych hospital."

Andy immediately rues leaving his wallet on the coffee table as he slept.

Having no desire to join Clete in jail, Andy crosses his fingers and takes the pills. An hour later, his eyes are twitching, his face swollen, his hands shaking, and drool occasionally escapes from the corner of his mouth. But he still has the hiccups. When Gloria's mom calls to chat, Andy has to retreat to the bedroom, so his hiccups won't be heard in the background.

Later they watch as Channel 10 follows up the hiccup holdup. They even interview a doctor who walks them through the causes of hiccups and tells them more than they ever wanted to know about the vagus nerve.

"Hic," Andy says. "Your mom suspect anything?"

"Naw, she's been in denial about me since I won a beauty pageant as a 10-year-old. I can do no wrong."

"Must be nice. I was more of a 'can't do anything right' child."

"I imagine it was tough, growing up in Clete's shadow."

His brother had been the quarterback, the prom king, which makes his current situation all the more perplexing to those who don't know him the way Andy does.

Sunday, they stay home. Andy usually calls his grandmother on Sunday afternoon, and he knows she will take offense if he fails to. However, he can't, not with the hiccups. So, he sends her a text message, claiming he has a sore throat and can't talk. Of course, she wants to take him to the hospital immediately, and it takes quite a few exchanges of messages before he can convince her that he isn't that seriously ill.

He spends most of the afternoon hiding in the bedroom closet, pillow to his face to muffle the hiccups, when Gloria's mother shows up unexpectedly and insists on cleaning the kitchen--cabinets, refrigerator and all.

Finally, after her mother leaves, Gloria comes into the bedroom and dons a black silk pants suit and red heels, carefully arranges her hair, applies some makeup.

"You look fantastic," Andy says.

She undoes a button of the top, unleashing another inch of cleavage. "It never hurts to look good when doing business."

Never having done business, Andy takes her at her word.

"While I'm gone, stay here; don't go wandering away, OK? We don't need you to get caught."

"There's one thing," he says. "If I don't show up at work tomorrow without calling off, they'll fire me. And I can't call, not with the hic hiccups."

"You want me to call off for you?"

"That's not acceptable unless you're in a coma."

"So, I tell them you're in a coma."

"Right. Then I hic show up tomorrow."

"Then deal with it," she says. "I have other things to worry about."

"You sure you don't want me to come along? I could be your driver hic if you need a quick getaway."

"I don't want us to be seen together and end up in the slammer because some crime nut hears you hiccup."

The solution to his work dilemma comes to him when he picks up his iPhone and remembers the recording app.

After experimenting for a few minutes, he is able to record part of a call-off message, stop the recorder, hiccup, turn the recorder on, and complete his message. He has to try it several times before he gets the timing right so there isn't an awkward pause in the middle. Since no one is in the office before 7 a.m., he will be able to leave his message on the answering machine.

Gloria calls an hour later. "He's not here yet, and I'm just killing time. So, I had this thought. You could visit a doc-in-a-box clinic in Indianapolis for your problem and no one would suspect anything. Why don't you get your car and drive there tonight? It's only a four-hour trip."

"I don't know," he says. "My car's ten miles from here, and I don't know if it's up to a 400-mile round trip."

"Jesus," she says. "Do I have to hold your hand every step? Just do it."

After hiccupping through the next hour, he decides that Gloria's idea has some merit, although it will require him to hike to his car, and he'll have to do it after dark, so he's not recognized. He hasn't walked ten miles in a day since Boy Scouts, but he can't see any alternative.

His cell phone rings again at 8 p.m. He checks the caller I.D., ready to reject any of his friends or relatives, but this one is coming from the state prison. Clete calls him every week or so, to check on life outside. If anybody will understand his situation, he thinks, and give him some wise guidance, it will be his brother.

"Hey, little brother," Clete says. "I thought it would be nice to spend three minutes together."

Andy knows that the prison limits calls to three minutes, so he doesn't waste time. "I'm in hic a lot of trouble, Clete."

"Did you just hiccup?"

"Yeah. I've been doing it since Friday. You hic read about the holdup?"

"I saw it on television. What the fuck were you thinking?"

"I wasn't. It was hic Gloria. Remember her?"

"Remember her? What are you doing hanging around with my girlfriend?"

"She's still your girl?" Andy closes his eyes and hiccups three times in rapid succession.

"No, I suppose not. She's not the kind of girl that has any loyalty. How did she rope you into this holdup?"

Andy tells his brother about their relationship, about Dean, about the money Gloria owes him.

"And you've been dating for two weeks? Jesus, I always knew you were a little slow, but this time you've been a complete idiot."

"What can I do, Clete?"

"You're at her apartment? Good. Give me the address."

Andy does so.

"Now forget about walking across town to get your car. Any cop sees you sneaking around in the dark is going to be suspicious. Just hang tight while I think of something. I'll call you in the morning; I'm allowed two calls a week now."

Just talking to his brother reassures Andy. Clete has always been the smart one, the one who can figure things out. He'll know what to do.

Andy wakes on the couch at 1:00 a.m. to a pounding on the door. He turns off the television, praying it isn't the cops.

A crowbar is inserted between the door and jamb. The door pops open like a champagne cork, and in walk two men. Not cops. Andy scrambles to his feet.

The taller of the two is older, perhaps in his late 40s, with male pattern baldness adding to the peeved look on his face. He is dressed in unbleached linen with a mauve shirt, no tie, black patent leather shoes.

The younger of the two is dressed far more casually; a hoodie over a black t-shirt, baggy workout pants, red Chuck Taylors. He is short and muscular, with fists the size of banana bunches.

Andy stands at the end of the couch, his escape route cut off by the men. The older of two he now recognizes as Butch Dean. "What do you want?" he says.

"Where's Gloria?" Butch says.

"She's at the casino looking for you. She has the money she owed you."

"Is that right? I heard she was hanging around there earlier tonight. Then she started playing blackjack. They say she dropped around ten grand in less than an hour. Did she have any money except what she owed me?"

"Not much," Andy said.

"I'll be fucked." Butch stares at his shoes for a moment, his hand cupping his jaw. Andy feels a pang of pity for the man. Even a hood, he thinks, should be able to count on the people he deals with.

Butch finally sighs, then slaps his hands together. "All right then, back to business." He points to his companion, then to Andy.

Before Andy can prepare himself, the guy takes two steps toward him and unloads a fist to the kidneys that sends a screaming bolt of pain through Andy. He begins to crumple to the floor when the man follows with a left hook to his stomach that takes away his breath and brings that pain to a new quadrant of his torso.

Andy doubles over, but he is too slow to the floor to duck the man's right cross to his chin. His jaw breaks with an audible snap.

He falls into a kneeling crouch, then rolls into the television stand as the man kicks him hard in the ribs. "Oh

God," Andy mouths, waves of nausea and searing agony passing through him as he waits helplessly for the coup de grâce.

Instead, Butch kneels beside him and says softly, "You talk to your brother tomorrow, tell him thanks. We'll find Gloria eventually; she's too stupid to get away, and she's got to pay for what she did."

"Clete ratted us out?"

"You'd be amazed what a smart guy like Clete would do in prison in return for a few favors. I got a lot of friends I look out for there. No reason he can't be one of my guys."

"He told you to beat me up, too?" Andy is as hurt by the betrayal as the punishment he's been dealt. Even if he is sleeping with his brother's girlfriend.

"Oh, no. This was a favor. He asked us to help you get over your hiccups. Worked, didn't it?"

Scratch and Sniff

Jaclyn Adomeit

On the night Nathan was conceived, his father dropped seven tabs of acid. He'd told Nathan about it each and every birthday, over the warm glow of the candles, until Nathan was nine. The summer Nathan turned ten, his father headed south of the border to warmer climes and a second family.

The headlights of Nathan's truck bounce over a pockmarked secondary highway, the light brushing dark canola fields. This far north, the radio sputters across stations. Spotty cell service, spotty roadside attractions, spotty people. The truck's technically a company truck, and Nathan's job title is technically Hot Shot. A title that means he drives whatever fits in a half-ton up and down Highway

63. The name of the job is the wrong side of dumb. Should have been Straight Shot. As in, yes sir, let me drive whatever the hell you want in a straight shot from point A to point B.

When Nathan was a kid, when his Dad first fled south, before he knew what acid was, what it felt like, Nathan would blame his father's compromised sperm on many things. When Nathan didn't get fractions in eighth grade, had to have been the acid. When his stomach curdled at even a glug of milk, those damn tabs.

It shocked the shit out of him when, at sixteen, he took acid for the first time, camped out at a buddy's dad's hunting property. By that point in his life, Nathan had cleared three and a half bases with two girls, but the acid made the female body an alarming thing. He had come forth from a body like that, escaped mewling from a hole. For months he couldn't so much as grab a tit. But the desire came back and the acid came round again, along with the pressed pills and powders, crystals and weed. Not everyone was ready to gamble a night on hallucinogens, but if that was a service someone wanted, it was a service Nathan could provide.

A grasshopper splats against Nathan's windshield. He pulls a long tug on the washer fluid and leaves a smear of guts. On northern summer nights, he fills up the windshield fluid more often than the gas tank.

Nathan won't admit it out loud, but sometimes he likes the job title, likes the way it sounds when he rolls it over his tongue, when he says it aloud over the buzz of late-night radio. Hot Shot. Like Big Shot. Reminds him of his mom's old Billy Joel records.

The straight shot part makes the extra curriculars of Nathan's job easy. He brings in specific parts for specific tools, sample equipment for when the oil leaches into places it shouldn't, and he keeps one cooler separate: standard issue blue like the others but with a Jeb's Oilfield sticker on either side. It's a marker as clear as when the men in camp leave kernels of popcorn outside their rooms: an invitation for wandering prostitutes, daylighting as cleaners. With this marked cooler, Nathan grants wishes. Steve, his guy on the inside, asks for coke, crack, crystal, oxys, H, Adderall, Dexedrine, methamphetamine, and like magic it appears inside the false bottom of the cooler. Nathan only makes drops when Steve is on shift—twenty on, ten off—but it seems to keep the boys in this oil camp, all two thousand of them, sufficiently sedated.

Steve will be waiting for Nathan tonight, a truck parked in the back corner of the camp lot. Nathan will lift the cooler onto Steve's tail gate, take one from Steve in return. Nathan won't even count the money. The boys out here believe in karma, believe in the lucky ghosts of oil and gas. The ones that will lead you to screen your well in the right geological formation so it spurts; the ones that will let a valve slowly leak acid gas into a ditch and take four guys to the grave with an invisible hand. Spirits. Where you put your faith and time, there'll be energy.

Nathan pulls up to the camp security gate, beneath the fly clogged glow of a safety light, and sees it's Ruth on duty. Ruth wears more eyeshadow than a drag queen, and all for a border shack post in a security vest.

"Evening." She spits the word.

"It's a nice one," says Nathan.

Ruth purses her lips like he's offered her a pickup line.

"New paperwork for everyone. You'll need to sign this before you drive through."

"Pretty girls are always looking for my autograph."

Nathan knows it's a cheap line, but Ruth's smile makes him feel like he's accomplished something. He reminds himself that he's only giving out the remarks to keep her searches sweet, short, and surficial.

"Don't get cute." Ruth's smirk rides her laugh lines. "If you need time to read it through, you can pull over to the side lot. No need to cram up the gate."

Nathan stops listening. The top of the clipboard has a title in bold dark letters.

Random Alcohol & Drug Search Protocol.

All staff are required to sign a search consent form before entering the facility. Those that don't sign the consent form, are not authorized to perform work.

Do or you're broke, thinks Nathan. Nothing quite like bankruptcy to motivate a man to relinquish some basic rights. He pulls into the lot beside the security gate.

Nathan skims through the document.

Sniffer dogs. That's what the paper is for. That if a circus-trained pup howls at his bumper, he's going to need to undo his belt, bend over, and say thank you very much to a two-finger salute.

Nathan wonders if they'd already found some of his goods within the camp. Well, they always find some. Kick a couple guys out of the facility every few months, blacklist them. That is, until they need drillers or pipefitters bad enough to clear the mark from their name.

Maybe they'd found all his goods. Found Steve. Made Steve rat. Maybe Steve's texts this afternoon were all a set-up.

Nathan heaves a double breath. Paranoia is what gets people caught. The most reasonable explanation is that a couple guys got busted, and the corporate ass-monkeys rolled out a new health and safety policy. Health and safety, more like liability management.

Nathan has two choices. He can sign this paper—and fucking soon so he doesn't look suspicious—or he can turn around and be guilty before a dog even whiffs his nutsack.

Nathan presses his pen to the dotted line. Random meant random-ish. They probably needed to get the dogs in place, get them trained. Nathan would probably never see so much as a tail.

He hands the clipboard to Ruth with a smile. The corners of his lips twitch.

"Great. When you pull through just follow the pylons. They'll direct you into a lot with the dogs and handlers."

She slides the window shut, and Nathan stops breathing. A truck behind him honks. Nathan tries to suck air past his Adam's apple. He sinks his boot onto the gas.

Right past the gate, the concrete barriers start. Nathan rounds the corner to find a snaking line of pick-ups, semis, and supply vans. All waiting for their chance beneath the generator-powered spotlights.

Three lanes, each with their own set of dogs, stretch across the gravel road. Each dog has its own handler in a bullet proof vest, like some terrorist is going to pop out of the forest and shoot up the place. The vests are probably another policy. Health and safety.

The semi in front of Nathan pulls into a stall, engine off, steps out. One guy leads a dog. It trots, sniffing the bumper, the tires. It completes one round of the truck, two. A second handler leads a dog to the driver. It circles the man. He stands, arms raised to the night sky, the dog snout deep in his ass crack. The pup backs off, turns to the handler, takes its treat. The driver doesn't balk until the guard on the sidelines shouts at him to move his rig.

In another lane, a dog perches at the bed of a truck, sniffing the same spot over and over. It sits, ass right on the gravel. Four security nobodies stream forward, open the tail gate, dig through the guy's tools, his bins, his garbage.

They are going to knock Nathan to the gravel road and peel him wide. Turning back, having Ruth suspect something forever, would have been better than this. He tries to calculate the amount he is carrying well over the weight to be charged with trafficking. These pricks probably have such a hard-on for police that they'll try and ring him through, not just take the stuff for themselves. He reminds himself that the goods are packed in the false bottom of the cooler, triple wrapped. That in the same bin, there's a decoy delivery of methanol and Fast Orange, stuff that smells, standard clean up goods that every guy uses to dissolve the bitumen off his boots. Steve came up with the whole shtick after Nathan's first couple drops. Apparently, an unmarked cardboard box wasn't discrete enough. Steve had ordered the matching coolers, slapped the labels on, and thrown in the cleaning products for good measure.

If they had found the other false-bottom cooler, Steve's cooler, they would know what Nathan's was right away.

The semi in front of his truck pulls away. A lady guard, so small Nathan could punt her clear across a football field, waves him forward.

"Evening, ma'am."

"Please exit your vehicle."

The rent-a-cop pulls Nathan's door handle, swings the steel panel open, holding it wide, like Nathan's a debutante.

He unbuckles his seatbelt and steps into the night.

A spasm starts up in his leg, just behind the right knee. He wonders if one of the oil spirits is telling him to run, telling him to go now. He reminds himself to stay put. Don't indict yourself: innocent until proven otherwise.

The bugs are thick in the night air, swarming the heat of Nathan's breath. He wants to pull his t-shirt over his nose, keep the six-legged shits from laying eggs in his nostrils. Instead he stands, tall and scowling.

A bald guard, his muffin top squelching out the bottom of his bullet-proof vest, starts toward the truck with a dog on a short leash, the man's hand tight on the chain. The dog's nose penetrates the gaps in the truck's rims. The front grill. Nathan tries to think of everything else that is in the back of the truck: gasoline, diesel, methanol, anti-freeze. That shit has got to smell. The dog's coat bristles as it huffs at the gaps around the doors, probably keen for the crumbs of Nathan's burger stop, his peanut grease fries. Nathan watches the handler, tries to see if the man flinches so the mutt will give signal. One good pooch and he can search whatever he wants with reasonable cause.

A second dog bounds toward Nathan, tongue lolling out from its mouth. The thing would be cute if it hadn't been brainwashed. The dog can sniff Nathan's nutsack all it wants. Nathan keeps his eyes on the one rounding the truck, snout deep in the back wheel well, taking its fucking time.

The handler stands so close that Nathan can smell his sour breath. Like the guy just gargled with French onion soup.

The dog sniffs at Nathan's right pocket, his left, and it sits its ass down on the gravel road.

Nathan tries to think. Is the dog just done, just tired?

"Positive signal." The handler pulls a treat from his pocket, offers it up to the dog. It crunches in the buzzing twilight.

Nathan meets the gaze of the officer. Wants to say, how about you go fuck yourself.

The lady guard walks in from the side. Now it's two on one, three on one with the mutt.

"I'm going to need you to turn out your pockets, sir."

Mosquitos peck Nathan's ears. A black fly lands on the guard beside him, takes a bite out of the guy's forearm. He swears, swats, leaving a streak of blood against a matted forest of arm hair. Nathan should have read the document he signed. Should have looked at what he was agreeing to. This was not probable cause. The handler probably tapped his boot and the dog sat. A treat-triggered search warrant.

Nathan reaches into his pockets, pulls out his keys, his wallet, turns out the cotton so lint blows away in the night air.

The lady plucks them out of Nathan's hands, holds them up to the dog. Flies buzz around the pooch's lolling tongue. It takes a brief smell of the wallet. As it sniffs the keys, it whines, scratching at the road.

The guard clicks on her radio. "We're going to need a swab room."

"Number two's all yours, Jean." The words crackle out. Someone orchestrating this whole thing. Someone watching.

Words traffic-jam behind Nathan's teeth, honking at one another to spew out.

"You blind? My keys aren't made of meth."

"We're still going to need to give them a contact test. Policy." The lady guard opens Nathan's key ring, separates the truck key. Doesn’t even ask, just pries Nathan's things apart. "An officer will supervise the inspection of your truck. I'm going to need you to come with me."

She hands the single key to the guard with the dog, pulls a plastic bag from her pocket, and dumps Nathan's keys and wallet inside.

Nathan wants to grab the bag, grab the key, get the fuck out of here. They've got nothing on him. He looks at where his truck is parked: concrete barriers on either side, a lifting steel beam in front. He wouldn’t get out without property damage, without this bitch chasing him down, without the cops hauling him in.

The lady guard starts toward an ATCO trailer, acting like she knows Nathan doesn’t have a choice.

Gravel crunches beneath Nathan's boots as he follows.

The guard's steps are sharp and sure, the stairs up to the trailer clanging beneath her feet, her hair tied up in a bun as tight as her ass. Four doors line the side of the trailer, tucked at the edge of the road. Four little rooms to take away a man's humanity.

The clang of Nathan's boots on the steps fills the night. He looks back toward his truck. Still a clear view to the vehicle, less than fifty yards. The mutt's at the back bumper now. Nathan forces his face straight, forces his breath steady. If the guard asks about his red cheeks, it's a hot night. Nathan's tired. He needs to get back to Edmonton, not be held up by this fascist shit. The mosquitoes form a haze beneath the trailer's lights.

"In here." The guard gives him a flat stare, light reflecting off her shiny forehead.

Nathan wonders if she gets paid by the catch. If every guy she tags means a big, fat bonus.

In the room sits a single chair. A plastic table stands along the back wall, lined with swabs, bottles, vials, and a box of blue gloves. A camera blinks in the corner. The only other door in the room bears a sign that says Washroom. In the place of a door handle, the hole is a taped over piece of cardboard.

"Seat's all yours."

Nathan knows he's better than this, stronger than this. He isn’t a bull being led to slaughter. He's a person, not a prisoner. All she has is a stinky set of keys.

"Been sitting all day." Nathan leans against the wall, looks out the window, back at his truck.

"Suit yourself."

The guard places the plastic bag on the table and slips on two blue gloves. She pulls a small slip of paper from a box, opens the bag, pinches his keys between her fingers, and rubs the paper on the key-fob. The guard lays the sheet in a petri-dish and pulls out a syringe.

Outside, the dog noses the dust on Nathan's bumper, pokes in and out, sniffing, taking it in. At any moment it's going to put his ass down on that gravel. The twitch in Nathan's knee sharpens. If that dog puts its ass down, if that fat rent-a-cop runs in here, Nathan is going to shrug. He's going to say, so what; he's going to keep his face poker straight until they pull out the coke and crystals from the fake bottom of the cooler. At that point, those aren't Nathan's things, just a load he's hauling for a shipper. These idiots in their Kevlar costumes are going to have to talk to the distributor and the receiver: Nathan is just a middle man.

The dog huffs and puffs at the corner of Nathan's tailgate, the handler holding close on the chain. The lady guard droppers liquid onto the paper in the petri dish. Nathan can see the paper from the corner of his eye: scarlet dots bloom across the white surface.

She pins her hands to her hips, scowls down at the paper.

"Sir, I am going to need you to take a seat."

Nathan is ready to stand his ground by the window. He's ready to say, make me.

The dog paws at Nathan's tailgate and sits its ass down on the road.

Nathan's stomach slumps. Bile heaves at the back of his throat.

"I can bring another security team member to assist with this process. Is that something that I need to do?"

Outside, the dog's handler waves a couple guards over. They drop Nathan's tailgate.

Nathan evaluates his options. He can run out there, and do what? Tackle the dog? Have three of these idiots flatten him to the gravel? The lady guard with the petri dish looks like someone took a dump in her high heels. If she found trace coke on the keys, he doesn't know what's next.

The plastic chair is cold as he lowers himself to sit. He tries to listen to the voices outside, but they're drowned out by the hum of the fluorescent light.

"Now what do you think all these pretty colours mean?" The guard holds out the red-splotched sheet, like it's show and tell.

Nathan's shrug comes off sharp. He rolls back his shoulders and slumps into the chair, arms crossed. He wonders if the camera has a mic. If her boss is watching. If some guard is knocking his fist against the underside of a desk staring at a screen.

"This shows that there are traces of marijuana on your keys."

Nathan lets out a snort. He nearly breaks into a full chuckle but stops at the look on the guard's face. Weed? This woman isn't calling the cops in about pot smudges. The trace is probably from one of the other Hot Shot drivers. Nathan never loads pot into the camps--shatter maybe--but no weed. You don't need a dog to smell weed: it stinks shit up from a mile away. Plus, the pay to cargo-size ratio is pitiful. Nathan tries to think of the last time he even touched pot. He keeps his piss as clean as possible. When he does coke, it's out of a system in forty-eight hours, max. None of this pot, fourteen-days shit. If they want to try and blacklist him for pot, if that's his ticket out of here, he will take it with a smile.

"I guess you got me. Pot on my keys. Probably the same thing on the wallet. One strike policy, right? Guess I better get in my truck and get out of here."

The guard dishes out an eyebrow raise. Nathan wants to ask if she's working it for the camera. The shouting outside is still minimal. He's sure he'd hear something if they found the false bottom. That dog will hopefully take its time, sniffing around the ten coolers, the twenty boxes in the back of the truck. It can sit all he wants. This is Nathan's out, and he's taking it.

"Seem a bit quick to leave us. Anything else we need to know?"

Nathan wants to say that the shit she doesn't know would knock her tits off. Silence is the solution here. No comment.

"No, ma'am. I get that pot's against the corporate policy. I'll take my keys and go."

"The next step on the A&D procedure procedure—the one you signed—is a piss test." The guard nods toward the washroom door. "We don't discharge from the facility without a positive sample. That wouldn't be fair."

Nathan understands what she's getting at: he leaves now, refuses to whizz in a cup, he might as well be guilty. A refusal to piss is as bad as a hot test.

"I'm sure the trace on your keys is transfer from something else. Someone else. Why not give us a sample? You piss clean, no mark against you."

Nathan considers the keys lying on the plastic table. Considers grabbing them and rushing out. He's still going to need the truck key back from the other guard. He thinks back to his recreational activities from the last weekend. Today's Thursday. A couple lines at the rippers last Friday. He's way more than clean.

"I piss in a cup and I'm free to go?"

"If the test strip is clean, you're good to leave."

Nathan stands, walks to the window. The guard doesn't stop him. Outside, they've got a couple boxes pulled out of the back of Nathan's truck, letting the dog take a good huff at each side of the cardboard. He reminds himself to play nice.

"Give me the cup."

The guard takes her time, looking through drawers, inspecting the seal. She pops off the orange lid and hands Nathan the cup.

"You'll have to leave the door open a crack. No funny business. Not that you could do anything. No water hooked up. Just fill it up to the black line, rest can go in the toilet."

Nathan pries open the door. Nowhere to set the cup but the splotched ring of the seat. The tank lid is missing. Bone dry. Nathan leaves the door open a sliver. The guard stands right there, chin up, back to the door.

Nathan just needs to get this done, get a strip that reads clean. It's going to be fine. It's going to take more than this to fuck Nathan over.

He drops his zipper, holds the cup.

Nothing. Not a drop.

He breathes deep. Waterfalls. Running taps.

The guard coughs, scratches the back of her neck.

He tries to force his mind out of the room, out of this piece of shit situation where a woman is waiting to hear him piss. He pictures driving out of here, giving the whole herd of cop wannabes a one finger salute and kicking up dust. The image lets him breathe in and relax. He fills the cup to the line, lets the rest drain into the toilet. Nathan zips up, pushes open the door.

"And I'll take that." She grabs the cup in a blue-gloved hand.

Outside, the guards have picked up the pace. Two more rows of boxes on the ground. Nathan can see one side the blue cooler, the one with the Jeb's Oilfield sticker, still in the back of his truck, tucked between two others. He's going to have to Tetris all that shit back in before he can leave. All the boxes are crammed up behind his back tires. He just needs to get out. Have the strip read clean. Get outside, show them the clear test, rub their faces in it. Tell them this is not probable cause; their corporate piece of two-ply be damned.

The guard dips a test strip into the cup of piss. The thing's as wide as a business card, words scrawled in little black letters, little paper windows beside each word.

"So, what's it say? It read clean?"

"We'll know in ten." She leans against the table, folds her arms.

Nathan's hands curl into fists.

"Ten what? Minutes?"

"An easy ten minutes. You're welcome to take a seat." She looks at her watch.

The dog finishes rounding a box. One of the guards, steps towards the truck, stomach bulge shaking. He grabs onto a handle of a cooler, the one right next to the Jeb's cooler, slides it out of the truck, and puts it on the ground.

"I'm done with this fascist shit." Nathan steps forward.

The guard places a blue-gloved hand on the door.

"No need to lose your cool. We're nearly done here."

"I'm done now."

Nathan grabs his keys and his wallet from the table. The guard stands with her back to the door, her hand on her radio.

"You going to detain me?"

Red creeps up the woman's sharp chin, floods her cheeks. She steps from the door.

The metal platform clangs under Nathan's boots. The big guard is grabbing the handle of the Jeb's cooler, pulling it out.

"Hey!" Nathan shouts. He runs down the steps. The other guards unhook Tasers from their belts.

Let them shock him. Health and Safety would have something to say about zapping a man who's only walking toward his truck.

Nathan grabs the other handle of the Jeb's cooler. The guard on the opposite side doesn't step back, keeps his grip.

"This is invasion of privacy."

"Son, I am going to need you to wait over there, take a seat on one of the boxes. You're on corporate property and this is corporate policy."

There is no way the guard is older than Nathan. Just because this guy ate his own family and looks like Christie Brinkley after a binge, he thinks he's older than Nathan. Nathan wants to tell the guy that since he isn't at risk for having a coronary emergency—like some people—he will stay standing.

"I'm packing up my truck and I'm leaving. Where's my key?"

The guard tugs on the cooler, trying to free it from Nathan's grip, to get it toward the dog, to have the little fucker sniff and scratch and sit his ass down on the gravel.

Nathan tugs back.

The sturdy handle, the one that has been so trustworthy during three years of pass-offs to Steve, three years of loading up, shipping out, snaps in two. Nathan stumbles back, broken plastic in his hand. His heel catches on one of the cardboard boxes. He spills over, falling, the gravel scrapping his palms.

He watches the cooler tip, fall off the side of the tailgate. It smashes to the ground with a crunch. The false bottom compartment cracks wide. White powder, wrapped beneath layers of cellophane, glows in the light of the generators.

A handler walks forward, a dog beside him. It sniffs at the cracked open side of the cooler and sits.

Go Fish

Brent Nichols

Jerry was fishing illegally, and should have known no good would come of it. He was at his favorite spot on the Little Big Bend, where an overpass kept the rain off and hid him from prying eyes. There was an eddy where the river ran quiet, making a pool where the water looked deep but was actually pretty shallow. Trout loved that pool. He was trying to tempt them with a hand-tied fake bumblebee when something big dropped over the railing and hit the water with an almighty splash.

He swore and dropped his pole, and tires squealed somewhere above him as the offenders lit out fast. Jerry got up, grumbling, to retrieve his rod.

And froze, staring at a man in a pinstripe suit tumbling along the bottom of the river.

He went in after the guy. Straight into the water, which was damn cold. Didn't even take off his shoes. He was proud of that impulse, later when everything went to shit. He did the right thing, there at the beginning.

Only it didn't help. His first thought, that some fool had jumped over the railing, faded as he saw the thick chain looped around the man's arms and legs. The guy wasn't struggling, either. He just bumped along in the current like so much driftwood.

The water, cold enough to make Jerry cuss under his breath, almost touched his balls by the time he got a fistful of the pinstripe jacket. He dragged the man into knee-deep water and hauled his head up until it was clear. Then he waited for the man to inhale.

Nothing. The guy's head flopped to the side, limp as laundry.

"Dammit." Jerry tried to get his hands under the man's armpits, then settled for grabbing the chain instead. He got the guy up onto dry land, and stood over him, staring, wondering what to do.

Somewhere in the back of Jerry's mind an unworthy thought briefly raised its head, a fantasy of a rich dude, grateful for the rescue, giving him a fat reward. The man looked rich enough – his waterlogged suit was pretty nice – but any gratitude had departed along with his soul. The man was obviously dead.

"Shit," said Jerry, telling himself he was saddened by the tragedy and not pissed off that he'd waded into a cold river for nothing. He looked down at the body, thinking about mortality, thinking about life and how it can just end.

It didn't take long for thoughts of a more prosaic nature to intrude. The man looked well-heeled. If he had a wallet on him, well, it wasn't doing him any good now, right? Jerry patted the guy down. No wallet, no cash, just a set of keys and a cell phone ruined by the water. Jerry thought about taking the suit, or at least the jacket. The guy was pretty small, though. Downright scrawny. And stripping a corpse?

Creepy.

Jerry stood, shifted his weight, and watched a stream of water flow from a hole in his left sneaker. His gaze drifted to the dead man's feet. The man wore black dress shoes, beautiful leather things with fancy curlicues on the toe caps. They looked brand new.

They looked just about the right size.

He looked around. There was no one in sight. He looked at the body, and he looked deep inside himself. Taking clothing from a dead body had to be crossing some kind of line. But shoes were just shoes, right?

They fit like they'd been made for him. He laced them up and took a few experimental steps. Then he smiled, grabbed his worn-out sneakers, and chucked them into the river.

The smile faded as he pondered the question of what to do next. Call the cops? There might be some kind of a reward from grateful family members.

He looked down at his feet, where the frayed cuffs of his jeans touched the hand-stitched leather of his new shoes, and imagined walking into a police station to report how he found a shoeless corpse. No, that wasn't going to fly.

A quick glance at the river showed his left sneaker still afloat, vanishing downstream at a pretty good clip, and he swore. Unless he wanted to walk to the cop shop in the tattered remains of his socks, he wouldn't be reporting this to anyone.

"Dammit." He clambered up the bank to his favourite rock and sat down. *I guess I'm done here. I should be thankful for the shoes. I should go.*

He stayed, though. He sat there, staring at the body, listening to a quiet little voice in the back of his head whispering about opportunity. A man was dead, and only Jerry knew. Well, Jerry and whoever dumped him over the railing. He wasn't sure yet how that was going to enrich him, but something was bound to occur. He just needed time to think it through.

The pinstripe suit was pretty dirty by the time he got the chain off, and the man was nice and light without it. Jerry tried to get him in a fireman's carry, failed utterly, and settled for grabbing him by the ankles and dragging him. A hundred feet from the overpass was a tiny doorless hut used by ice fishermen to keep firewood dry. He put the corpse in the back of the hut and draped it with a ratty old blanket. Then, deep in thought, Jerry walked home.

#

He woke to the sound of bagpipes several hours later. He was stretched out on his couch, the TV still on, and he spent a confused moment fiddling with the remote, trying to hit mute. The TV was already muted, though.

Finally, he stumbled across his tiny apartment to the kitchen, which wasn't a separate room, just a fridge, stove and sink a whole four paces from his bed, where he traced the mystery music to a bowl full of rice covering the dead man's cell phone. He pulled the phone out of the rice and stared at it, telling himself he shouldn't answer. But his finger seemed to move without his control, swiping across the glass.

"Hello?"

"Sam! Sam, is that you?" It was a man's voice, sounding relieved and annoyed. "Where have you been? Are you okay? Mom's been worried sick!"

Something drew Jerry's gaze to the television, where a tearful older woman wrung her hands and spoke into the camera.

The text bar underneath identified her as "Elizabeth Tremblay, Mother of the Missing Man".

"I'm not Sam."

The voice on the phone immediately turned hostile. "Who are you? Why do you have my brother's phone?"

The woman on the TV wore quite a nice necklace, Jerry noted. He couldn't have said what the stones were, but they sure did sparkle. He didn't know a lot about women's clothes, but her dress had an expensive look. She was in front of a McMansion, one of those big yuppie castles with lots of stone and wrought iron.

She clearly had a few bucks.

"Let me talk to Sam." The dude was trying to sound menacing, but he was too scared to pull it off.

Jerry weighed his options, took a deep breath, and said, "No."

"Who are you?"

"J-" He stopped himself just in time. "I'm … Jay."

"Who the fuck are you, Jay?"

Jerry, doing his best to sound like Tony Soprano, said, "I got your brother. You want him back, it's gonna cost you."

"Fuck." There was quick, muttered conversation in the background. Then the man spoke again. "How much?"

"I need … ten thousand dollars." As soon as the words were out of his mouth Jerry wanted to snatch them back. These bozos had to be worth millions. Ten grand was chump change, and it made him sound like a punk. He flushed. *I shouldn't have answered the phone. I need time to think.*

"Ten grand?" Was that relief in the man's voice, or amusement? "We can do that. Is a cheque good?"

"Very funny," Jerry growled. "Cash is good. Or I can start sending you fingers in the mail."

"All right, all right. We can get you the cash in an hour or so. Where do you want it delivered?"

Shit. I should hang up. Think of something, then wait for them to call back. He said, "Uhhh …."

"Take your time." There was definitely amusement in the man's voice now. "I'll wait."

"There's an overpass at the river," Jerry snapped. He gave instructions to his fishing spot. "Chuck the money over the railing. Make sure you don't hit the water, or your brother goes in after it."

"Fine, fine. Like I said, we need an hour or so. Maybe an hour and a half."

"I'll be waiting," Jerry said. "Don't make me wait too long. When I get bored, I like to cut people, and the only person around is your brother."

Thirty minutes later he was back at the river, his fishing pole under his arm. Once he got off the phone with the dipshit brother, the plan had come together in his mind with wonderful clarity. Ten grand was pathetic, and he knew he'd kick himself for years, dreaming of the money he could have had. But there was an upside. The family would pay without hesitation. He'd be free and clear with more money than he'd ever had in his life.

He took a seat on the riverbank a couple hundred feet downstream from the overpass. This was the really brilliant part of his plan. He was in plain sight. He looked completely innocent, just a guy trying to catch some fish. If the family got cute, or if they called the cops, no one would give Jerry a second glance. If someone tried to set up a nasty surprise, Jerry would see it all from a safe distance. He could just reel in his line and walk away.

"I'm a genius," he said, and settled himself on a stump.

It was late morning, and he shivered, wishing he'd brought a coat. Cloud covered the sky from horizon to horizon. He shrugged. What was a little hardship for a cool ten grand? At least it wasn't raining.

Five minutes later, the first fat drops hit him. He swore, turned up the collar of his shirt, and told himself to suck it up. As the rain came pelting down in earnest, though, his gaze kept shifting to the overpass and all that lovely dry ground just a couple hundred feet away.

I can't stay here. Not in pouring rain. It looks suspicious. If I was just an innocent fisherman, I would totally get up and run to the overpass.

"Oh, fuck it." He stood up, reeled in his fishing line, and broke into a run.

It's better this way. I can't see shit in this rain. No one can. I'll be in and out like a ninja. Gone before my bag of money has time to bounce.

He ran, hunched over, cold drops pelting his shoulders and the back of his head. His thighs were soaked, and his new shoes, which had never completely dried out, were wet again. Then his foot came down and raised a cloud of dust, and the barrage of icy impacts against his shoulders ceased. He was under the overpass. He stopped, sighed in relief, and straightened up.

A wiry little man in a charcoal suit rose from behind the rock where Jerry usually sat to fish. He reached Jerry in two quick strides and sank a fist in the pit of his stomach. Jerry doubled over once again.

Standing up was beyond him. He twisted his head to the side and watched as a second man rose from behind the rock. Both men were short and skinny and dressed like lawyers. It was only when he looked at their eyes that he started to get scared. They had cold, pitiless eyes. They had eyes like his ex-wife.

One man took a little transistor radio out of his pocket, turned it on, and set it on the rock. Loud rock music came belting out. The other man produced a white handkerchief and began wrapping it tightly around the knuckles of his right hand.

"Wait." Jerry's voice came out as a sad wheeze, completely drowned out by the music. "Wait, you don't-"

Something hit his kidney. It felt like a hammer driving a nail into his back, and he screamed, collapsing to his knees. Gravel scraped his forehead as his body curled forward.

It got worse from there.

At first, he felt every blow. Later the impacts blended together in an incomprehensible storm of pain. Jerry squeezed his eyes shut and floated in a sea of agony, while an angry voice shouted questions and impacts rocked his body. Then came a shocking cold, and a terrible sense that he was drowning.

Jerry's eyes flew open. A stream of water was pouring into his face. It stopped, and he blinked his eyes clear. He lay on his back. A man stood over him, holding one of Jerry's new shoes. He'd been using it as a pitcher.

"Where's Sam?" The man looked at the shoe in his hand. "Is this his shoe?"

"You piece of shit," said the other man, and a toe slammed into Jerry's lowest rib. It was a good, solid kick, and Jerry hissed, unable to get enough breath to scream.

"Where is he?" A foot came down on Jerry's left hand, the pressure slowly building. "Where's my brother?"

"I pulled him out of the river! I saved him." Jerry inhaled, the air rasping and moaning in his throat. "Well, I tried to save him. But he was already dead."

The pressure on his hand didn't let up, but it didn't get any worse either. "What the fuck are you talking about?"

Jerry babbled out the whole story. "He's in a shed. It's just over there. I never hurt him; I swear. I pulled him out of the water. I tried to help him."

"Check it out."

The foot remained in place, the pressure on Jerry's hand never wavering as the other man hurried away. He was back in a minute. "There's nothing in the shed but firewood."

"What? No! I put him in there, I swear! I tried to-" The shoe ground down and Jerry's pleading voice became a scream. He kept on screaming for several more minutes while they worked him over. He discovered that the first beating really wasn't so bad. It was nothing at all.

After a time, the fog of agony began to recede. It was still quite awful, but it was stable now. There were no fresh injuries, no new damage. Jerry tried to open his eyes. The left one remained shut, but his right eye opened a little bit.

He was face-down on the ground, staring at one of the hand-stitched shoes he'd stolen from the corpse. It lay scuffed and abandoned on the ground a couple feet away. Something moved against his buttocks and he spent a bad moment wondering exactly what his new friends had in mind.

They weren't molesting him, though. They were filling his pockets with rocks.

Fists clutched the shoulders of his shirt, pulling the fabric tight against his armpits. The other man took him by the ankles. Jerry struggled and found that his hands were tied behind his back. Someone grunted, and Jerry rose a couple of feet in the air.

"Last chance, buddy. Tell me something useful."

Jerry said, "Ah, shit."

They started swinging him from side to side. Back and forth he went, and then one man started to count down. "Three, two, one!"

For a sickening instant he was airborne. Then he landed in cold water and sank.

It wasn't as bad as he might have expected. The worst of the chill faded in a few moments, and the cold took away some of the pain in his mangled hands. He lay face down on a smooth bed of stone with the current dragging insistently at his shoulder. He couldn't see much point in struggling, but his body started to thrash in spite of him as he fought the urge to inhale. His upstream shoulder rose a few inches, and the current caught him and flipped him over.

Lying on his back meant lying on his broken hands. That wasn't too comfortable, so he sat up. His body turned in the current until his feet pointed upstream, which meant the water pressed against his chest and face. Curling his body against the current took some effort, but he was frantic to keep his weight off his hands. The last of the air in his lungs burst forth in a cloud of bubbles as he finally got himself sitting upright.

To his utter astonishment, his head broke the surface.

An inner voice told him to take a quick breath and duck back under the water before the GQ Twins spotted him. He didn't care, though. Just holding his head above the surface took all the strength and all the courage he could muster. He spent a minute just sitting there and breathing.

When he finally turned his head, the two men were gone. The transistor radio still sat on the rock, blaring music. He decided he'd take it with him when he got out. It wasn't ten thousand dollars, but at least he'd get something for all his suffering.

The song ended and a DJ came on, bitching about the rain. Jerry ignored him, trying to figure out how he could hitch his way closer to the shore without drowning himself. Then he froze, his attention arrested by the tinny voice coming from the little speaker.

"… has just been found. He's alive, too. I'm getting an update from our reporter in the field. Listen to this."

The man who spoke next sounded so much like the GQ Twins that Jerry instinctively flinched away from the radio. “I almost died.” The man sounded badly shaken. “But some Good Samaritan saved my life. Someone must have pulled me out of the river, because I woke up soaking wet. I was in a little shack with a blanket over me. Someone took me out of the water, put me in the nearest shelter, and then left before I could say thank you.”

“There you have it,” said the DJ. “Sometimes it seems like there’s nothing but bad news, but here’s proof. There are still heroes in the world. And good deeds don’t go unrewarded. Sam Tremblay says if his benefactor will come forward, he or she will get more than just a heartfelt thank-you. There’s a cash reward.”

The music started up again as Jerry began to laugh. His body shook, and a fat rock tumbled out of his hip pocket. He began to slide, pushed inexorably downstream by the current. The stone beneath him sloped downward, and he slid faster.

He was still laughing as his head sank under the water.

Johnny Money

Steve Passey

I sit and wait in the coffee shop, waiting for Patty to come and see me. He called me up on my cell and told me "Have I got a fuck of a story for you," and I tell him where to meet me 'cause I know if it is that good it can only be about one man: Johnny Money.

I like a latte' (I know, I know, bitch coffee but I like it). Milk, sugar, and caffeine, but with espresso black as death poured into froth white like a carnation. Patty comes in no time all. Patty calls himself "Patty Bones" because his name is Patrick Bonny. No one else calls him that. You can't give yourself a nickname. Everyone knows the rule. Everyone but him calls him "Patty". He should be careful, especially around Johnny. If Johnny hangs a nickname on you it sticks. Every time he introduces himself as "Patty

Bones" let me tell you this: He is just one word from Johnny Money away from being "Patty Pussy". All right, two words. But he's here and he gets his latte', (no espresso, bitch coffee for real,) and he tells me: "So Johnny called me the other day."

"What'd he call ya?" I say. Hey, he calls himself Patty Bones. You know I am gonna take my shots.

"Ha ha, fuck ya" he says, and then soft and serious, "He asked me to come with him to find Ricky."

This is serious. Ricky is Johnny's half-brother. Ricky is only ever "Ricky" because Johnny won't let anyone nickname him. Ricky and Johnny couldn't be more different. Johnny is short and strong and built like a bull. Dark hair and darker eyes. And then there's Ricky. Ricky is tall and blond and freckled. Always looks like he just stepped out of a sunny day. Ricky's like his mother – the two had different mothers - in more ways than one. Johnny's mom died when Johnny was born. The old man must have been lonely, or just didn't know what to do with Johnny, so he married Ricky's mom. She said she was Irish, but I think she didn't know what she was. Tall, blonde and freckled, just like Ricky now. Johnny was a little more than two when she had Ricky. She was a bad one. Drank and smoked reefer, as they called it in those days, and pretty much left Johnny and Ricky to watch for themselves. They were young. Too young to be left on their own. One too many vices one too many times and Johnny's dad threw her the fuck out. She was on the street, and she packed it in and went and ran reefer with some bad people, and then wound up whoring for some worse people, until she fuckin' died and turned up in a morgue. She'd been a Jane Doe there. She had no family of her own, but someone down there recognized her. So, the morgue called and Johnny and his dad – not Ricky – went down and identified her. The old man wouldn't bury her or nothing. No funeral – no marker - no nothing. "Fuck it," he said to the guys at the morgue. "Throw her out with the trash. Throw her busted-up ass on some busted-up pallets and strike a match. You do whatever the fuck it is you guys do but not on my dime. All I'll say is that it is her. She's dead. Goodbye and good riddance." Johnny didn't say anything, just walked home with the old man. I don't know what they told Ricky about his momma. I haven't a clue. He must have been around eight when it happened. So, Johnny grew up like the old man, dark and close, and Ricky grew up like his momma, tall and good looking, and always fucking things up. But Ricky had a good heart and he always had Johnny to look out for him. Johnny told me once that his mother was perfect: She had gone heaven to look out for him, but Ricky's momma was so bad that Johnny had to look out for Ricky on this earth because Ricky had no one in heaven to look out for him. It's hard to always look out for someone on earth.

"What happened?" I ask, "What did Ricky do now?" I did not say, "What'd Ricky fuck up now" because I don't want something like that to get back to Johnny. Johnny watches out for Ricky, and if you say anything like that about Ricky it's like you are insulting Johnny.

"He won money in the lottery," said Patty, matter-of-fact and looking smug, waiting for me to press him.

"How much?" I say. I almost shout, and I have to look around to make sure no one heard. Fuck me; I am like a little kid. Softer again I hiss, "…how much?" But I know by the way I say it my eyes are big.

"Ten large," Patty says with a shrug, leaning away, looking into his (bitch) latte. "Not too big, not too small, but just the right size, if you know what I mean."

I do know what he means. Guys like Johnny; they win a lot of lotteries. By which I mean they buy the winning tickets, at a modest premium, because winning lotteries is their legitimate source of income. That way the Feds can't nail 'em on tax evasion. They have something to show and a place where it came from. So, in our little corner of the world ten large is perfect. Because ten large is more like twelve large once you factor in a modest premium. Fuck, Ricky is family and Johnny looks out for him, so for Ricky that's more like fifteen large. That's a nice premium. Higher than that fuck-up Ricky can count, but I don't say it.

Patty looking at me brings me back. Something is not right. Patty has got that look, that smile, like he knows something I do not. But he wants me to guess. He wants to draw it out. Fuck you Patty Pussy I think, but I ask anyway:

"So, why did Johnny Money call you?"

"I already told you, to find Ricky."

The fucker. He won't let me have it.

“Why would Johnny need you to find his own fuckin’ brother?” I ask. “And Ricky should be looking for Johnny no? There is a premium there for him.” I can’t play along anymore, I am not getting it, and fuck him he can just give it to me, or I’ll finish my latte’ (with espresso) and be done with it. Patty’s stories are never that good anyway. He’s a hanger-on. A wannabe, a…

“Because Ricky don’t wanna be found,” Patty says, no smile now, all-knowing and all-serious and I answer my next question myself:

“Cheryl Anne?”

“Budda-Boom,” Patty says leaning back again, his shoulders open, he’s given it up to me now and the subject is open for discussion. You see, Johnny may not like family business being discussed out in the open, but it’s not like Patty told me. I guessed it.

“That fucking crack-whore Cheryl Anne.” I don’t ask it, I say it. As a statement, it stands.

“More than you know, brother,” says Patty, looking pensive. But it’s an act. The only reason Ricky would run from his brother and fifteen large would be to hand over that winner to Cheryl-Fucking-Anne. And Johnny Money? Well, Johnny ain’t gonna stand for that.

Ricky and Cheryl Anne have had a thing since forever. They have had it since grade school – which was the last time she actually went to school. Ricky was enough of a jock to glide by. Hell of a football player, but he didn’t have the marks for college. Didn’t have the desire, really.

Ricky just wanted things to be easy. And way off in some college town Johnny wouldn't be there to look after him. Johnny told me once the only thing Ricky ever really did that pissed him off was not go to college. All the other shit Ricky got into or fucked up – that was just Ricky being Ricky. But college was his chance to not be Ricky and he didn't even try.

And you know what else? Ricky wouldn't leave Cheryl Anne. I'll say it. Even Johnny would say it. The way Johnny looked out for Ricky: Ricky thought he looked out for Cheryl Anne. At least Ricky was grateful to Johnny. But Cheryl Anne just shit on Ricky and Ricky always came back for seconds. And thirds. And fourths. And so on.

Now that I have guessed my way in, Patty can tell his story. He quits drinking his (bitch) latte' and talks with his hands like a man reading the sports scores from a paper and trying to describe the play that lead to what he is reading.

"So, Johnny calls, and you know me - I go. I ain't gonna say sorry I am busy to Johnny Money. If it was my mother's funeral, I would say no, but Johnny wouldn't be asking. He would know if it was my mother's funeral. And note that at this point I don't know anything about any lottery ticket. I just know Johnny's looking for Ricky. So, I go. I ask Johnny where we are going, and he doesn't say. We get over to the avenue and he hails a cab. "Butterface's" he says. That's the Russian peeler joint. I am thinking this is good. Ricky likes peeler bars, likes peelers really, and it's a good place to look. Plus – there are peelers."

I stop to agree with Patty – naked chicks are never a bad thing – and nod him on.

"The cab pulls up and the cabby tries to wave Johnny's twenty off, but Johnny won't have it. You know Johnny, he always pays, never lets people comp him. He is honest and forthright in all of his transactions. Johnny will kill you before he will disrespect you. That's his rep. Everybody knows. We get out of the cab and walk into the club. This is early afternoon remember, and there are not many people in there. Igor, that oversized bouncer they have in there, that jacked-up dude with that fucking vein in his arm that looks like a knot? The kind they say you get from animal steroids? He stands up when Johnny walks in and doesn't say shit. None of the 'You gentleman have a good time' bullshit those juice-monkeys say when they really mean, 'Please, please, please touch one of the girls so I can hang a boot-fucking on you and prove my love to whatever lap dancing lesbian is paying my rent for this month.' Not a word. Igor stands up and stands back, and even though he's taller than Johnny he looks small. So, we walk in."

I need to clarify for myself. "Who owns Butterface's? The Russians I know, but which Russians?"

Patty is happy to oblige me. "The Ukrainians actually. The money is in Europe. But the guy who is in charge is a guy everyone calls Super Heavy on account of that was his weight class. Not that bodybuilder ass-shaving shit. Serious stuff like in the Olympics. I have never seen the guy, but I have heard he is huge. He makes Igor look like piece of

Chihuahua crap. That's how big he is. He runs the place like it's Europe too. No class at all. He basically comes in every so often and takes all of the money in there that day. He comes in, empties the tills, shakes down the dancers, beats seven shades of shit out of a few mouthy patrons – Igor's job is to throw them out after Super Heavy rolls them. Then he's gone for a while, until he comes back. Rinse and repeat. That's no way to run a business if you ask me. Look at the way Johnny runs his shit. Johnny has process. Johnny has order."

"So, Super Heavy is pretty huge, and the Russians are still a bunch of fucking goofs," I say. "But back to Johnny and Ricky."

"Oh yeah," says Patty, "So Johnny and I walk over to the bar where Viktor is. Viktor bartended there before the Russians even owned it. They kept him on when they took it over because Viktor was one of their own. I sit at the stage, but not too close to Johnny. I do not want it to look like I am listening to his business, but I have to be close enough to watch everyone coming in the door, and still keep an eye on the girl on stage. Business and pleasure hey? And she was a good one too. The Russians bring 'em in from Russia. That's logical. Sixteen, seventeen years old and harder than frozen rock these girls. Nice titties too – small ones, set up firm and high. They remind you of the first piece you ever got. They wave it at you and you tip. You tip bigger and you get a lap dance, you tip real big and …"

"Is this story about Johnny and Ricky or is it about you paying twice the going rate to nail a peeler?" Fuck, he calls himself Patty Bones. You know I am going to take my shots.

"Ha ha, fuck ya," he says.

Patty and I – we have a rhythm to our speech. We practice.

"So, I watch the girl dance, and I listen to Johnny and keep an eye out. Johnny asks Viktor 'Is Cheryl Anne still dancing here? And Viktor doesn't say a damn thing. Just looks at Johnny and shakes his head. So, Johnny asks, 'Viktor, is Cheryl Anne dancing anywhere?' Viktor just shakes his head again. I am starting to worry. You know how Johnny is about Ricky. Just give it up Viktor, old friend, is what I am thinking. But Viktor doesn't give. He has this hound dog look in his yes, like he's trying to beg Johnny not to ask, but it's all about Ricky. Johnny is gonna find out come what may."

"Was Johnny packing?" I ask. I am thinking to myself that going into the other guys turf, a peeler bar run by a jacked-up psychopath no one knows anything about save that he's big, foreign and crazy – I'd be packing. Packing large.

"I didn't ask, and you wouldn't either," says Patty "But I doubt it. One time I asked Johnny about packing and he said that it's a bad idea most of the time but a good idea some of the time. I asked him why that was, and he just said, 'Think about it.' So, I did, and this is what I thought:

If you pack all the time, everyone knows you are packing then they are packing too, and the shit is going down all over and it's not good for business. Plus, who wants to get pulled over for a seatbelt violation and get busted for packing? But if you never pack word gets around that you are not a hothead. So that when you are packing and if the shit goes down? Let me put it this way: You're packing."

I have to give him credit. "That's pretty smart Patty."

He shrugs. "Not my idea. Johnny Money's. Anyways, Viktor shakes his head one last sad time and says in a thick Russian accent 'Super Heavy is coming. I cannot help you now.' I notice that the girl is gone, the waitresses are gone, the DJ has left, and the song has ended. Fuck me, it got quiet fast. All of the patrons have gone. Even Igor and his animal steroid vein are gone. Everyone checks their watch. Well, me and Viktor check, not Johnny. Johnny doesn't wear a watch. 'I am not a slave to time,' I once heard him say. But everyone blowing Butterface's at the same time on a Friday afternoon? Even the suits? How fucking ridiculous. And speaking of ridiculous, Viktor never had an accent for the first forty years of his life but once the old country Russkies showed up he's harder to understand than the rest of them. But I digress. No sooner do Viktor and I look up from our watches than the shit goes down."

"Goddamn!" I say and slap my hand on the table for emphasis, rattling my cup and Patty's (bitch) latte'. "Viktor was packing!"

"No, no, no; fuck no," shouts Patty. He's excited too now, and people are looking at us. He makes himself be quieter and says, "I mean, fuck if I know, 'cause the moment he said that Viktor hits the ground behind the bar. I mean it. Takes a dive. You know those Russians, they're divers. Soccer, hockey, bartending. I come up to the bar and try to look over the edge. I mean, what the fuck? But Johnny is looking at the door. And that's when I hear it. That po-ta-to, po-ta-to, po-ta-to of a big-ass bike. Vintage. You know the sound. And it gets louder and louder and louder until BANG! Right through the fucking front door."

Patty is standing now, his arms out wide. Everyone is looking. Fuck 'em, I can't wait for him to finish and Patty doesn't need to be asked.

"The biggest fucking Russian you have ever seen rides through the door on a Harley and slams into the stage like a fucking bomb! You should fucking see this guy. He's actually wearing a Viking helmet. With braids"

"Fucking braids," I say. I am rolling in my seat. The rocket strike of the Russian's bike has blown me off of my own ass and this is second hand, a day after it happened.

"Fucking braids," Patty says. "But wait it gets better. The guy gets off of the bike and gently, so gently, sets the helmet down on the seat. The braids hang to the floor. And I tell you, you have to see this guy. He is fucking huge. I mean, at least six-and-a-half-feet tall. Three hundred twenty-five pounds if he's an ounce. You know that vein Igor has in his arm? From all of the animal steroids? Well this fucking guy has two. In each arm. And these veins have veins. And this guy and his fucking veins walk on over to the bar. He doesn't even look at Johnny. He pounds his fist on the bar and says, 'Get me a fucking drink!' in a thick Russian accent. It's not as heavy as Viktor's, but more real. Like an executioner's voice. I swear to fucking God Almighty just talking about it and I feel like pissing myself!'

"Nah, that's just that bitch latte' you were sucking on," I say. Hey – he calls himself Patty Bones. But he ignores me this time and goes on.

"So, the Russian looks over the bar, trying to spot Viktor with me and Johnny looking over the edge with him. But Viktor is wedged tight down there behind the bar and no one can see him. It's like he disappeared. Then Johnny – cool as a cucumber – says 'It seems our host is indisposed. Let me pour you a drink' and very formally and politely he takes a half-empty bottle of Stoli and grabs a glass. Without a fucking word the Russian grabs the bottle from Johnny, takes the glass and pitches it behind the bar to shatter in a million pieces, squeezes the spigot out of the bottle, then lifts it and chugs it. He chugs the whole fucking thing – a half a bottle of primo swill – in 5, or maybe 6 gulps. The whole time his expression never changes. But Johnny's does. Let me tell you, Johnny's does. You know what I mean. You have seen it. His expression is no expression. You know what I mean?"

Indeed, I do. You don't disrespect Johnny Money because he does not disrespect you. Johnny will kill you before he will disrespect you. So, prepare to die.

“The Russian finishes the bottle and fires the fucker into the rows of bottles behind the bar. Fucking fires it. If anyone on the Sox had an arm like that they would be in champagne rehab. It’s all broken glass and running liquor in there, and I get giddy for minute thinking poor old Viktor down there might drown in a lake of spilled hooch on a bed of broken glass.”

“It would serve him right for diving!” I say and Patty goes on, oblivious to anything I say now. He’s back in Fallujah now with this story, with guns blazing going house to house, room to room against the Muj.

“Johnny says – cold now - with no expression, ‘Would you like another?’ and the Russian looks Johnny up and down, up and down. It’s that second that feels like a year – you know what I mean? The hands are ticking on the warden’s watch?”

I know it, I know it. I wasn’t even there, and I can hardly stand it.

“The Russian says, ‘I’ll pass. I heard Super Heavy is coming so I’d best be getting on out of here.’ He walks off, puts on the helmet with those fucking braids, saddles himself back on the hog, and backs out. He doesn’t fire it up until he hits the street. Po-ta-to, po-ta-to, po-ta-to getting farther and farther away. The music comes on again, the girl comes back out on stage, and Igor’s back on his little stool looking smaller yet in comparison to Johnny and that guy on the bike. Johnny and I keep our eyes on the door. After that who knows what the fuck is going to come next?

But Viktor is up again, and he says without a hint of an accent, 'Cheryl Anne is not here and she's not dancing. But if you go to the old Pavilion Hotel off of the avenue – the old one – you will find her.' Johnny slides Viktor a twenty for the Stoli and Viktor tries to waive it off. Johnny waves it right back and says, 'Viktor, I don't have time to argue. I have to go. I hear Super Heavy is coming.' Johnny cracks himself up with that one and starts to laugh even as we walk out Johnny is still busting a gut laughing. I don't laugh at all; I don't mind saying. I should laugh at Johnny's joke. It is funny, but I am still thinking about that guy coming through the door on that goddamn big bike. When we get outside into the sun the first thing I do is look down to see if there is stain on the front of my pants. Johnny's still laughing and he hails another cab.

"Word and true? I gotta go because Super Heavy is coming?" I am laughing too now, laughing hard. This is a good story.

"Every word," says Patty, "Word and fucking true. Some shit you just can't make up. No matter how wild it sounds. It's called 'The Axiom of Improbability' but I ain't a professor, I do not know how to explain it other than to say: Fuck it. It happened just exactly so."

I have no comment. Axiom of Improbability? That fucker Patty has been reading again. I'll take that up with him later. "Go on," is what I say.

"Anyways, Johnny quits laughing when we get to where the cab will go no farther. We get out, and right away we head down the alley. You know the old town. It's not like it is up here now. When I say alley, I mean crawlspace – wide enough for one man to walk. There is no such thing as two-way traffic in those places. Alleys now are like streets were 100 years ago. Better, actually. This is a one hundred-year-old alley like back when they really were places to fear. It is dark in there too. The sun never shines there. Johnny is hustling, really moving, and I gotta hustle to keep up. We make some lefts, some rights, and I am totally lost but Johnny's making a beeline for somewhere. You know Johnny, he's the man, but even if he wasn't, I'd have stuck with him by this time because there is no goddamn way I could find my own way out. And before you know it, we are there."

"Where?" I ask.

"Hell's waiting room I guess," says Patty and the way he says it I know he's serious. "I mean, the building is condemned – but the back door is solid metal and can't be part of the original. Even without Johnny knocking on it I know this has to be a place, so for here it must be the place. Know what I mean?"

I nod.

"So, Johnny knocks and a voice comes out of the door 'Who da fuck dat?' it says, and Johnny says 'Johnny Money!'"

"Damn!" I say. Johnny never refers to himself as "Johnny Money". He just says "John" actually. Just like you can't nickname yourself you can't easily refer to yourself by your nickname all the time without coming across as a bit of a cock.

"Damn, is right" Patty says. "We're on the same page on that one. But no sooner does he say 'Johnny Money' than you can hear the chains and deadbolts slide and turn in a mad scramble and the door opens. A little Chinese woman no bigger than one of that Russian's veins. 'Mr. Money,' she says, 'I am very pleased that you have come by. How can I help?'

'Cheryl Anne,' he says. 'Is she working here?'

'She's not working right now,' says the little old Chinese lady. 'She's resting.'

'Where?' Says Johnny, and I can see he is not patient.

'The same room where she works of course,' says the little Chinese lady. I can see she's like Viktor, she doesn't want to answer so she's hoping Johnny won't ask."

'I am going to speak to her,' says Johnny, 'it won't take long.'

'Mr. Money, you put me in bad way,' says the Lady. 'I can't say no to you. You are Johnny Money. But you are not customer, so I can't say yes.'

"When she says this Johnny's face starts to lose all expression again. I see it. But more importantly: She sees it. She's thinking. She's grinding, and she has no expression, but she's not mad. She's scared and looking for an answer. Who can blame her? But then she comes out with it:"

'Maybe you don't come here to see the girl? Maybe you have come here to have your tea leaves read? Maybe you have come to have your fortune told?' She's smart this little old lady is, smarter than I am for sure. Johnny catches on right away and hands her a twenty. The hands tick on the hangman's watch then Johnny looks at me. Fuck it. I am outnumbered. I give her a twenty. She looks hard at the twenties, and after a short second or two says, 'Your fortune says that you were never here.' She points at the stairs to her left and walks away down the hall. Fucking broad, she'll probably iron Johnny's twenty and frame it, and then go wipe her moldy old ass with mine. The Chinese are superstitious about money."

"So, I hear!" I have to agree about superstition and money. "She made a good call though. What next?"

"We go up the stairs. The boards are new and strong but unfinished – the place smells like sawdust. At the end of the stairs is a small landing and a door that actually has a hole kicked in it. I guess the repair money started and ended with the stairs. So, Johnny knocks on the door, softly now, and not like a goddamn cop breaking in. Doesn't bother to look through the hole to see who is on the other side, doesn't worry about that shit. He just knocks. Three times. Knock, knock … and then knock. And then after a second she speaks 'Come on in Ricky' and I know we've found her.

"Cheryl Anne." I say, definitively.

"If she's surprised to see Johnny and not Ricky, she tries not to show it. She's sitting in this little chair – one of those that sit in front of a make-up table. But all her make-up and shit – it's all on the floor lined up against a wall. The back of the chair is against the wall too. There's a foam mattress beside her and a toilet and sink just across form that. There is a thing like a sawhorse in the middle of the room, only too tall for that, a black metal tripod, like for a camera. A plastic sheet is on the floor. No windows. Daylight comes in only through cracks in the wall, and it smells like piss. It like an Old Testament Hell this place is."

"Old Testament!"

"And as bad as this place looks, Cheryl Anne looks worse."

I have to think back to what Cheryl Anne used to look like. Back in the day – there is no denying it – she was hot. She grew up fast. She grew up tall. She had this red-blonde hair and blue eyes, but dark, like she was always pissed off. And she was. But she had a laugh too, a wicked laugh that made you laugh with her and she laughed often. She had those small high breasts that Patty said the Russian girls had and she never had 'em done. Any problems Cheryl Anne had that needed fixing started and ended with her soul, if she had one. If she did, she would long ago have traded it to get high. Even if it was just once, for just one high, because nothing else ever meant anything to her.

But Patty brings me back again. "Cheryl Anne is fucked up man. Black eye that looks like it was put there by a baseball bat. I mean it – you could not do that by hand. Her head is shaved, and you can see scars in her hairline – those wide scars you get from when you should have got stitches but decided to tough it out. Split lip too, and fucking cigarette burns. Fucking cigarette burns! On the inside of her arms. A fucking line of them. She's wearing a man's wife-beater too and that's it. That and a leather dog collar. And the wife-beater - it's all stained too – blood I bet, or worse. Fortunately, it hangs to beneath her waist 'cause believe you me, I do not want to see where those burns end. Its god-awful I tell you. God-awful. Johnny and me, we just sit there looking at her. So finally, Cheryl Anne says 'Hello John. I did not expect to ever have the pleasure again. Whatever brings you here?' And then she giggles. She's got that hungry junkie look in her eye – the one they get in their sober moments just before they plan their next score so they can forget that they saw themselves in that sober moment. And Johnny says just, 'Cheryl Anne.' And she giggles again and then stops giggling all at once.

'So, what do you want Johnny?' Cheryl Anne says. Johnny says nothing.

'You want to fuck, Johnny? Fuck your brother's girlfriend? It's going to cost some. And if your boy there wants to watch he's gotta pay same as."

Johnny still says nothing.

Cheryl Anne keeps going. 'You want oral? Oral, Johnny? It's gonna cost some more. And if your boy there wants to watch, it's gonna costs same as.'

Johnny still doesn't respond.

Cheryl Anne motions to the plastic sheet on the floor. 'You want me to pee on you Johnny? Well! I never figured you for that, but I'll pee on you. It does nothing for me, but

I'll pee on you. It'll cost a little more yet, though. If your boy there wants to watch … you know.'

Johnny says nothing. I can see he's looking at Cheryl Anne's face though. Her black eye. Her split lip. All her problems, and Ricky's, right there in front of him, in her face.

'Oh Johnny," Cheryl Anne says, 'You want this? You mean this?' She points at her eye, then her lip. 'I don't know how I missed it. I'm not even surprised. Well yes, Johnny, you can have that. But it's going to cost more. A lot more.'

Johnny turned to me then and said, 'Ricky ain't here. Let's go.'

Cheryl Anne lost it then. 'Tell Ricky,' she says. 'Tell him Johnny. He'll be here as fast as he can. I know he loves me. Tell him I love him too. You know he loves me too. More than anything. Tell him to come and see me. Tell him to bring his money and if he's nice to me maybe – just maybe - I'll let him watch when they take their shots. Because I love him, he can watch. He still has to pay though. I need them more than I love him. Tell him Johnny. Tell him that. He'll come anyways.'

Patty gets quiet. I can see he's lost in remembering it, looking around that room, at Cheryl Anne, hearing her speech. "So, what'd Johnny say to that?"

Patty thought a minute and said without looking at me "Nothing. He turned on his heel and walked out of the room, slowly, no rush. He walked past me and started down the stairs his feet heavy on the new boards like he didn't care if he was heard. Thump thump thump. But I waited and watched Cheryl Anne and the moment – the fucking moment he was out of her view she comes running forward. She sprang up like an animal trying to pounce. Her one good eye – you know how she had those dark blue eyes – it looked like it was a fucking light. 'Fuck you Johnny! Fuck you!' She screamed, more spit than air coming out of her banged up mouth. 'You tell your fucking loser brother to fuck off and die too!'

Patty was quiet again for a while.

"Well, what happened?" I say.

Patty finally looks up at me to finish. "I left then, and last thing I saw was Cheryl Anne lying on the floor in that messed up shirt with her knees under her chin, her hands around her legs, rocking herself back and forth. I walked down the stairs and into the alley a little ways behind Johnny. It's late afternoon and the sun is starting set. And like I said before, we got to hurry on out because that's a dark place and I don't want to be there at night."

"Jesus, Patty," is all I can say to that. Patty is quiet now and I excuse myself to go get us some more coffee. We need the break. I order the same for both of us, the lattes with the shot of espresso. Time for Patty to nut up and drink his latte' like a man. Especially after that story.

Patty doesn't complain about the espresso and then starts again. "So anyways, we walk out going the opposite direction. Good call on Johnny's part he knows not to go back the way he came."

There is something profound about that, I think. Knowing better than to go back the way you came. It's a metaphor for life, for getting to heaven. Johnny knows his shit by instinct I'd say, while the rest of us learn the hard way. Not that Johnny is a religious man. You know most of these guys are observant, if not devoted. Funerals, weddings, they go, they are always there. But Johnny doesn't do either. I once asked him – do you not believe? Why do you not go? And Johnny, more than a little annoyed with me said; "Of course I believe. So, I don't blaspheme. So, I don't drive. So, I don't have to go." Like it should be obvious, and you know? It should be.

Patty begins again "So we walk out and after some twists and turns we're back out on the docks. It takes a little longer and it's getting dark. Johnny says fuck all to me the whole time. Eventually we are back out under some lights and eventually we find a street and Johnny gets us another cab and we get in. We're back in the city. We drive and Johnny finally says to me, 'There is nothing you can do for Cheryl, Patty, nothing.' I think he said it just in case I was gonna go get all Ricky on him. It's a comment, it's an order, and it's true in every way. I wasn't really thinking of it – I mean – what could be done for Cheryl Anne anymore? And remember – at this point I still don't know anything about the lottery ticket. I just know we are looking for Ricky and he wasn't at the peeler bar (still a good bet I think; even if not this time around) and he couldn't have found Cheryl Anne (the next safest bet). But Johnny

Money's reading my fucking mind the whole time and he says,

'I know where Ricky will be. He hasn't found her and no one else will ever tell him where she is even if they did know. They know me too well. But let's not take a chance. We'll go to the Pier.'

"That's where the cab takes us. Johnny pays the cabbie of course, ignoring the guy when he tries to waive him off and tells him

'It's an honest occupation, take the money. If ever I need a favor, I will ask.'

"Johnny will never need a favor, hey? But that cabbie will always be there to do one for him if ever he needs. And so, Johnny's world goes round and round. When Johnny gets out, he says to me 'You're an expensive date, Patty!' and he laughs. He's as calm and as cool as he has always been. I can't laugh. I am still in Cheryl Anne's room."

"Have some more of that latte Patty" I say, "That's man-coffee there." Poor Patty, I can see I gotta get him though this, if I am gonna hear it all. And Johnny was right. There was nothing to be done in that dark room. Patty goes on.

"So, we walk the pier. You know it's not like in the old days. It's a yuppie paradise now, all bars and bistros and places like this. But it's nice and well lit. Colored lights. Funny hey? I used to laugh at that colored light shit but go to one dark place and all you can think is how pretty colored lights are. Johnny walks out to the last pier and there sitting on the little wall looking at the water away from the setting sun is Ricky. Sitting all alone and real quiet. I stop at respectable distance. This is family business. Johnny just stands there for a while. Ricky has to know he's there but he's not saying anything. Remember, at this point I don't know about the lottery ticket. Johnny called - I came. He doesn't owe me an explanation. When it's finally dark Johnny says;

'Hey Ricky. Been looking' for ya. How ya been?'

"Ricky takes a moment - a long moment – and then shrugs, but he don't look back. 'Hey Ricky' Johnny says, 'It's me, Johnny. Talk to me Ricky.' But Ricky still don't answer. Johnny's not pissed or anything. He sounds relieved, like 'Oh fuck, I found ya, I can sleep easy now,' and remember I don't know about the ticket. I think that this is the end of it. Johnny found Ricky, Ricky's in one piece; have a nice day Patty Bones."

I ignore the "Patty Bones". Fuck it – it's a fuck of a story and he can have it this once.

"But no one moves. And finally, Johnny says, 'You got something for me Ricky?' Ricky turns as if to say something, but then turns away again and says nothing. So, Johnny says again 'You got something for me Ricky? More insistent this time, but more like he is concerned, not all flat and unemotional like he's gonna kill Ricky. Not that that would ever happen, but you know Johnny's rep. Only Ricky would have immunity and he should probably not count on it.

Finally, Ricky says, without looking at Johnny, his eyes still on the dark water, 'Do you remember mom?'

Johnny is quick to answer

'Sure Ricky. I remember your mom for sure. But not mine, she died too young.' And Ricky is quiet again and then says, louder now, 'I remember when she'd be lost for a few days. You know how she would just get lost. We'd worry and worry and the old man, he'd get madder every day, and we'd worry until worry turned to fear. But then she'd come back again. She'd be happy and she'd cook, and we'd all eat together. She was a wonderful cook Johnny. You have to give her that. You know she was. Cooking made her happy. Her cooking made us all happy.'

"Johnny was quick to respond to that one too. He said, 'I remember being happy to eat.' Ricky goes on:

'I got nothing to remember her by Johnny. Nothing. Not even a picture. Not a scrap of clothing. Nothing. But I got the good memories Johnny, the good ones. You do too, you just won't admit it. I was thinkin' …,' and he trailed off and Johnny answered for him, quicker now.

'You were thinking what, Ricky? That you could make things right somehow, some way? How Ricky? How?' Johnny's still not mad. He's just quick. So, Ricky waits a minute, a minute to make sure Johnny's not interrupting him.

'I was thinking, you know, I'd get a ring, or something, and we'd move. You know, one of those college towns, someplace far away, where it would be easy for her. You know, easy. I'm a handy guy, I could do damn near anything, and we could just … get by.' I expected Johnny to be on him for this, on him like white on rice, and be harder than the back of your old man's hand. But Johnny said nothing. He said nothing for a long time. We all just stand there. The water has turned to night now, black. Finally, Johnny speaks:

'Ricky, you are my brother and you are all the family I got. We are the two sons of Anthony Ryan Monetti. And that's all the old man had. Our dead mothers? We are all our mothers had. Family, Ricky. We got a family of two. Have I not always taken care of you? A ring ain't gonna make it right. You can't fix her just like you can't bring either of our mothers back. For you, you can dream, but it's a dream. Give me the ticket Ricky; give it to me now, so I can take care of you in this world. Do not leave it to dreams.'

I have to interrupt. "So, this is the first time you heard about the ticket?"

"Yeah", Patty says, "and although at the time I did not know the amount he'd won. That came later, from reputable sources. It all fell into place. Ricky had some luck and was on the verge of fucking it up and Johnny had come to save his ass. God only knows if Ricky had been able to find Cheryl Anne. She would have put the ten large through her veins, nose, and mouth in about a week, and whoever is keeping her chained to a wall in that fucking hellhole would have shown up and killed them both. And then the real shit-storm would start."

"Word and true," I say. "Word and true. So, what'd Ricky do?"

"Well, it took a minute, but he swung around, got on his feet and came over and handed Johnny the ticket. The he went and sat back down and stared at the water."

"And that was that?" I ask

"Not really. Johnny took the ticket and put it in his coat pocket without even looking at it. The tension is out of all of us now. Me? I feel like I could use about a twelve-hour nap. But Johnny hasn't said anything to me, and I don't know: Should I stay or should go? So, I wait. Johnny goes over to Ricky and sits on the wall and swings his legs over the water like Ricky and puts his arm around him. I mean, big Ricky there and short dark Johnny, and Johnny cuddles him up like you would your kid. And Ricky starts to cry. It's a bad thing when a man cries. Ricky just cries, his back heaving and the air coming out of him in bursts, his voice like an animal's. And Johnny just sits there, his arm around Ricky, and holds him tight. You know Ricky, he was that guy. He could throw that football, hit that baseball, but he's just a kid really. He needs Johnny."

"He's lucky he has Johnny. But you are right, I won't mock another man's pain. It's a fuck of a story but it's a shitty thing. Do you think Johnny will give him a premium?"

"No."

But after a moment Patty reconsiders and says, "I mean, I doubt it. Really, what for? The ticket or the premium – in

Ricky's hands it goes to Cheryl Anne. The end result would be the same. And Johnny will look after Ricky somehow, some way. Always does. Always will. That's Johnny Money. Anyways, I was just standing there but Johnny hadn't forgotten. When Ricky's finally quiet he turns his head and says 'Thanks Patty. You need a cab?' I decline the offer of course, but I can go. So, I do. And I have not told anyone of this, except for you. All you are going to hear is that Johnny won ten large in a lottery. But now you know."

Patty is tired now, and the last latte is gone. Its dark just like when Ricky gave Johnny the winner. Time to go, I guess. But empty or not I gotta raise my cup and Patty his:

"To Johnny Money," I say

"Johnny Money," he says.

CEMETERY PLOT

Steve Brewer

It's hard to maintain your dignity when you're on your knees, watching another man dig your grave. I'd managed not to cry or piss myself, but I couldn't control the sweat that burned my eyes and soaked my white shirt.

The humid September air bore no hint of a breeze. It was so quiet in the cemetery I could hear gnats droning around my sweaty scalp. Every *chunk* of the shovel into the soft earth echoed around the clearing carved out of the woods for what Wayne Elrod insisted on calling the "nigger graveyard."

I'd recognized Gentle Rest Cemetery as soon as Wayne and his sidekick Lester McHugh opened the spacious trunk of Lester's '72 Plymouth and dragged me handcuffed and blinking into the midday glare. The isolated cemetery was at the end of a gravel road – at the *dead* end, we always joked – and I'd spent many youthful evenings parked out here, necking with girls who thrilled at the creepy surroundings.

Black folks kept the small cemetery mowed and well-tended, fighting back the encroaching forest and repairing occasional vandalism by local rednecks. Even the oldest of the weathered tombstones were clean and level.

The grave where I knelt had a gray marble marker that was shiny and new. The stonecutter must've had a policy of charging extra for punctuation. It read:

IGNORA PERKINS

Beloved Mother Wife Friend

Born 6 12 1924 Died 8 1 1986

I didn't recognize the name. Whites and blacks still kept themselves separate in this part of rural Arkansas. We were polite at the store or passing in daylight, but the courtesy covered a simmering bitterness that went back to slave days. Mrs. Perkins, whoever she was, no doubt had gone to her death quietly resenting white people. Now she was about to share her grave with one.

Wayne watched from the shade as Lester shoveled out the rich soil. Sweat dripped off the ends of Lester's Fu Manchu mustache and soaked his clothes. He wore faded denim bellbottoms and a yellow tank top that showed off the muscles in his tattooed arms and sunburned shoulders. On the front were scrolled the words *Bad-Ass Gym*, which made the shirt a relic. Bikers burned that gym to the ground years ago, showing people who the real badasses were.

Wayne Elrod didn't look like a badass himself, but he was the scariest little peckerwood I'd ever known, murderous and manipulative and mean. Wayne thrived on human turmoil, like a seed that only sprouts once the soil is disturbed.

He got rich quick selling weed, then promoted himself to local crime kingpin, dealing in drugs and moonshine and gambling and girls. He owned half the county and collected rent from the other half. Wayne mostly managed things by phone from his rambling house on the outskirts of town, but some jobs required a personal touch. My death apparently was one of those.

Shadows dappled Wayne where he stood under the reaching limbs of a catalpa tree, his eyes hidden behind mirrored sunglasses. He held his big six-shooter in both hands, occasionally turning the cylinder with a metallic click that seemed louder than the shoveling.

He wore Wranglers, a belt with a big silver buckle and a snug T-shirt as black as his slicked-back hair. A compact man, Wayne favored cowboy boots with stacked heels. They made him lean forward slightly, so it always felt like he was about to get in your face.

A lot of faces in southeast Arkansas carried scars from encounters with Wayne Elrod. He'd just as soon hit you in the mouth as eat supper, and most people were afraid to hit him back. Afraid they'd end up in a place like this, watching Lester McHugh shovel away the last few minutes of their lives.

"That'll do, Lester," Wayne said abruptly.

Lester hesitated. The hole was not even three feet deep. He chipped at the edges with the shovel, squaring up the corners. I appreciated his devotion to craftsmanship, especially if it delayed by another few seconds the bullet designated for my brain.

Wayne circled around the grave, coming up behind me as Lester climbed out on the opposite side.

"Normally," Wayne said, "I can't abide the mixing of the races, but this seems appropriate. You act like a nigger, betray your friends, steal from your betters. You deserve to end up in a nigger grave."

I twisted my neck around to look up at him. "I didn't steal anything."

Lester grunted. A laugh? A warning? His square face showed nothing as he hefted the shovel and examined the edge of its muddy blade.

"You take me for a fool, Rick?" Wayne leaned in close, speaking into my right ear. "You think you can steal my weed and sell it right under my nose?"

"I didn't steal—"

Whap! The barrel of the six-shooter cracked across the back of my skull. Wayne hadn't put much effort into it, but it still hurt like hell. I teetered for a second, nearly fell into the grave.

"You think I don't know my own weed? I been tracking that crop since the seeds were planted. That pineapple undertone in the smoke? Hell, boy, that's my *trademark*. I can recognize that smell when somebody's driving past on the highway, smoking a joint at seventy miles an hour."

I lifted my throbbing head and looked at Lester. No help there. He stared into the grave, waiting. He still held the shovel in both hands. I wondered if the plan was for him to do the honors. Why risk the noise of a gunshot, even way out here in the woods, when a shovel to the skull could handle the job? Would Lester do that to me? Could he? We'd known each other since grade school.

"A bale of my weed disappeared two weeks ago," Wayne said. "Forty pounds of pot, just poof. That don't sit well with me, of course, so I started asking around. I hear Rick Steen's suddenly got weed for sale. Primo smoke, way better than the skunkweed he's peddled in the past. And he's got volume, too, willing to sell *pounds* at a discount."

Still no breeze, but the sweat chilled on my body and made me shiver. Wayne knew more than I'd feared. He knew everything. Well, *almost* everything. Would telling him the rest do any good? Would it buy me more time?

"Where did you come by this premium weed, Rick?"

"A guy I know."

"What's that? Look at me when you're talking."

I could see myself reflected in the lenses of Wayne's sunglasses. I didn't look so good. Sweaty and disheveled, hollowed out by fear.

"I got it from this guy," I managed. "I didn't know it was stolen. I thought the guy was smarter than that."

Wayne cocked back the hammer of the big revolver, loud next to my ear, and said, "I thought so, too."

The pistol boomed. I snapped my head away and fell over onto my side next to Mrs. Perkins' desecrated grave. Before I'd even hit the ground, I could see I wasn't the one who'd been shot.

A red hole erupted in the center of Lester's chest, puncturing the yellow shirt right between the "Bad" and the "Ass." Eyes wide with surprise, he fell backward over the pile of dirt he'd made beside the grave. One long, ragged exhalation toward the heavens, and Lester was no more.

"Get up," Wayne said to me. "Can you hear me? Get your ass up."

Ears ringing, hands cuffed behind me, I struggled up onto my knees.

Wayne still pointed the smoking pistol at Lester, as if he expected the big man to rise and fight. Finally, he sighed and lowered his gun.

"Lester worked for me for better than twenty years," he said. "I loved that man like a brother. But I won't let anybody steal from me."

I knew better than to answer.

"If I'd shoot my good friend, a man I trusted for decades, just like that—"

He snapped his fingers.

"—imagine how easy it would be to put a bullet in you. I don't even *like* you. Never have. Slick Rick. Always acting like you're smarter than the rest of us. Guess you don't feel so smart about now."

I lowered my head and watched the sweat drip off my lank brown hair while I waited for the end.

"I knew it was Lester," Wayne said. "He'd been the good soldier for years, but greed crept up on him. He saw all this weed moving through the county and figured I wouldn't notice if some went missing. But, good God, forty *pounds*? How am I *not* gonna miss that?"

"I didn't know the weed was yours, Wayne. I only knew it came from Lester."

"Where the hell did you think he got it?

"I didn't ask. He cut me a good deal on five pounds, said I could pay him once I sold it."

"That didn't make you suspicious?"

"I wasn't looking at it like that," I said. "I was broke after my divorce. Ever since I lost my job at the Ford dealership, I've been getting in deeper and deeper. This dope deal seemed like a gift from Heaven."

"You interested in Heaven? I could give you a first-hand look at it."

Wayne pointed the big revolver at my face. I flinched. Never have I hated myself more than at that moment. I was no more than a cowering dog, quivering at the master's feet.

I forced myself to straighten my spine. If Wayne was going to shoot me anyway, I might as well act like a man. Maybe I could persuade us both that I wasn't acting.

I looked past the big pistol, focused instead on my reflection in Wayne's sunglasses. I was still flushed and sweaty, my white shirt streaked with mud, but my jaw jutted and my eyes were angry slits. I looked pretty formidable for somebody in handcuffs.

Wayne busted out laughing.

"Look at you! All puffed up, ready to fight. What you gonna do with your hands cuffed? Kick me in the ankle? Bite me? Hey, that's it. What don't you bite me?"

I didn't say anything. Too busy trying to look noble and brave.

Still chuckling, Wayne walked around the grave to where Lester lay splayed over the pile of earth. He bent over him and started going through his pants pockets.

I thought about running for it while Wayne's back was turned, but there was no way I could run fast enough to reach the cover of the trees before he'd shoot. Not with my hands cuffed behind me. Not in loafers.

I still dressed for the dealership every day, though I'd been unemployed for months. My dope customers thought it was amusing that I wore button-down collars and khakis and loafers. Most of the stoners didn't own a shirt with buttons. Their idea of formal dress was a plain T-shirt without a beer slogan on it.

Wayne stood, Lester's keys jingling in his hand. He walked around the grave and came up behind me. He rested the muzzle of the pistol against my neck.

"Be still."

My heart pounded. My mind projected the trajectory of the bullet, how it would blow out my windpipe and the arteries in my neck. A quick death, but dear God, it would hurt.

Wayne surprised me again. He unlocked the cuff around my left wrist. Before I could recover from the shock, he dropped the keys into the dirt beside me and backed away.

"Take off those cuffs."

I could barely get enough breath to speak. "Are you going to let me go?"

Wayne laughed uproariously.

"You're an optimist, Rick, I'll give you that."

Flushing hotly, I grabbed up the keys and undid the cuff from my other wrist. I thought about throwing the keys and the handcuffs at Wayne's face, but what would that accomplish, other than to piss him off more?

"Get on your feet, motherfucker. Somebody's got to bury Lester, and it ain't gonna be me."

My knees protested, but I stood up. Wayne kept the pistol pointed at me while he held out his other hand. I stepped close enough to give him the handcuffs and keys, then he waved me back with the gun.

"Go on around there. Push him into the grave and cover him up."

I didn't want to touch Lester's sweaty corpse. I went all the way around the dead man so I could get hold of the straps of his tank top. He was heavy – dead weight – but I managed to flip him over so he landed face-down in the grave. The exit wound in his back looked like a bloody mouth.

I paused for a second, breath catching in my throat, a shudder running through me from the contact with the dead man. I managed not to puke, but it was a close call.

"Get after it," Wayne said. "I ain't got all day."

My stomach heaved again as I dumped the first shovelful of dirt on Lester's bloodied back. I sucked up a deep breath and stabbed the pile of dirt with the shovel and tossed it into the grave, not even looking where it landed. I focused all my attention on the dirt pile, shoveling furiously until I was out of breath.

I paused, panting. The dirt had landed haphazardly, but Lester was mostly covered now, his clothes peeking through here and there.

Wayne stood across the grave from me, grinning.

"You think that nigger woman knows Lester's on top of her like that?" he said. "Practically fuckin' her, idn't he? Nothing in the way but some dirt."

I lifted another shovelful off the pile and tossed it onto Lester's legs.

"Save a little room in there for yourself," Wayne said.

While he guffawed, I leaned on the shovel and used my sleeve to wipe sweat and mud off my face.

After he got quiet, I said, "You're not going to shoot me, Wayne. I thought you were at first, but you're smarter than that."

He pointed the revolver at me, but I kept talking.

"You've figured out by now that I'm the only one who knows where Lester put the rest of that dope. You don't want to kill me before you get your hands on it."

Wayne smirked. "You don't know shit. Lester wouldn't have told a weasel like you about his secret stash."

"I was with him when he hid it," I lied. "He pulled off that five-pound chunk and I carried it away in a Hefty bag. The rest of the bale was still intact. Maybe he sold off some of it or—"

"Tell me where it is."

"I don't think so."

"I'll shoot you in the goddamned knee. Bet you'll tell me then."

"No, I'd come across this grave at you, even if it's on one leg. You'll have to shoot me dead. Then you'll never see that weed again."

"I can live without that weed. You, on the other hand, would be dead."

I shrugged my tense shoulders. "The way you tell it, I'm dead either way. Why should I help the man who's going to kill me? What's in it for me?"

Wayne said nothing. I couldn't see his eyes, couldn't tell what he was thinking. My brain was busy with the math.

"Even at wholesale prices," I said, "that dope's worth a hundred and fifty thousand dollars. Surely getting it back is more important than killing me."

"It's important to set an example," he said. "I don't, and I'll have every cocksucker in the county trying to steal from me."

"Isn't Lester example enough? Like you said, even your best friend isn't safe—"

"Don't talk about Lester. He'd still be alive if it weren't for you."

"I'm not the one who shot him."

"No, but you led him astray."

"He came to me—"

"He was faced with a temptation," Wayne said. "You were the devil on his shoulder, telling him to go ahead."

"It wasn't like that."

"You say that *now*. But you'd say anything now, wouldn't you, Slick Rick? Tell any lie to keep me from pulling the trigger."

"I'm not lying."

He extended his arm, pointing the gun at my gut, which set off a new round of mental calculations. He was only five feet away. The shovel was six feet long. Time was running out.

I swung the shovel like a baseball bat, so hard and fast that the blade whistled through the air. Wayne ducked backward, but I wasn't going for his head. I aimed for the hand holding the pistol.

The gun roared just as the shovel cracked against Wayne's forearm. The bullet hit me on the left side of the belly, tearing a hot hole through the flesh just above my waistband and spinning me halfway around.

Wayne's arm had a new joint in it between the wrist and the elbow. His hand still held the heavy pistol, but it pointed at the ground.

He screamed and bent over, clutching the broken arm to his chest, so both his hands were too busy to ward off the shovel, which I swung straight down like a sledgehammer. The blade cracked his skull and sent him tumbling into the grave on top of Lester.

Hot pain flared in my belly. I pressed against the bullet wound until the pain subsided a bit. My hand came away covered in blood.

Gutshot. I didn't have much time. It was a long drive back into town. Once I showed up at the clinic with a bullet wound, the cops would be all over me. I needed to cover my tracks.

I clenched my teeth against the pain and pushed the shovel into the dirt pile. I flipped the earth onto Wayne, who lay on his side, blood and brains dribbling out of his head, the mirrored sunglasses hanging crooked off his face. His blood soaked up the dirt, so I threw another shovelful. I kept shoveling, though the pain made me cry out at times.

I wasn't thinking clearly, wasn't thinking at all. I just wanted the bodies covered. Within a few minutes, Wayne was no longer visible and only a little dirt still remained scattered in the grass around the grave.

Breathing hard, I gave the mounded dirt a couple of pats with the shovel. Pain and dizziness washed over me. Blood had soaked my pants to the knees. Time was nearly up.

I dropped the shovel and staggered toward Lester's blue Plymouth, thinking: I don't even need to make it all the way to town. I can drive to the highway and flag down some help.

I fell against the front fender of the big car. Its metal skin was scorching from the sun, but I didn't have the strength to push myself away. Instead, I slid along the fender, leaving a red racing stripe of blood.

Falling into the driver's seat caused another wave of blinding pain. I sat there a moment, panting in the heat, trying to focus my eyes so I could drive out of there.

I reached for the ignition.

And that's when I finally thought of the keys.

Last time I saw the car keys, they were in Wayne's hand. He probably put them in his pocket while I was shoveling dirt onto his sidekick. That's where they remained. In his pocket. Under a foot of dirt.

Shit.

I crossed my arms on the Plymouth's big steering wheel and rested my head on my forearms. My elbow pressed against the car's horn. The horn echoed about the woods like the baying of a hound.

I didn't really expect anyone to hear the horn way out here. Certainly couldn't count on someone coming to investigate the noise and getting here in time. But it was my only hope.

I wondered which would give out first: Lester's car battery or me.

SOFT OPENING

Will Viharo

Ray Xavier—better known as X-Ray—was putting up the spectacularly lurid one-sheet poster for the Seattle premiere of *Cocktopussy: Tentacle-Testicles of Terror* in the outside display case. His favorite new song "Escalator of Life" blasted from the radio inside the lobby of the recently renovated and reopened theater, formerly an Art Deco palace called The Grand, now a porno-grindhouse called The Rabbit Hole. He then went inside to the tiny office and turned on the pink, bunny neon sign above the marquee. Just then the ominous clouds began to weep, making the venue seem that much more cozy and inviting, especially for patrons that were planning on wearing raincoats, anyway.

Next, Ray — a former burlesque emcee wearing his best vintage sharkskin suit and his black hair slicked back — ran up to the booth to check with Max, the pimply-faced young projectionist.

"How's the print?" Ray asked.

"It's almost brand new!" Max said. "So, it's fine. I just finished building it up, in fact."

"I was worried since it's coming off a three-month run in Times Square," Ray said. "And frankly, the distribution company seems a little shady to me. Mafia or something. So secretive and sleazy. We'll need to be careful about paying them, just to be safe."

"The Mob is infiltrating the porn racket big time, I hear," Max said. "That would be kinda cool though, right? To be in bed with real gangsters? As it were."

"You're totally romanticizing that milieu, kid. You don't want to mess around with those guys. I'm glad they didn't stick us with a totally trashed print, anyway, especially since this is our first night of business, however unofficial. First impressions count, especially when your main source of promotion is word of mouth."

"Well, my assessment of the print does come with a *caveet*."

"A *caveet*? What the hell is that, a side dish?"

"Huh?"

"You mean a *caveat*, you idiot."

"Insults are against union rules."

"Fuck the union. What are you trying to tell me, Max?"

"I can't promise the reels will be in order. They weren't numbered, so it was hard to tell. I tried checking to make sure the continuity was intact, but I won't know for sure until I run it once. If you let me do a trial screening, I could be sure."

Ray looked at his watch. “That’s what happens when they deliver the print the day the movie opens. Bastards. First show is in two hours. How long is this stupid fucking film, anyway?’

“Eighty-two minutes of non-stop fetishistic fornication, from what I can tell. So maybe it doesn’t matter if the reels are out of order? It’s not like anyone is paying any attention to the plot anyway, right? Still, I take pride in my work. It’s my responsibility and I’d like to get it right, so we don’t completely embarrass ourselves on opening night in front of paying customers. Nobody wants to patronize amateurs. Not even scumbags and perverts.”

“Okay, go ahead, but that’s cutting it close, literally, since you may have to rearrange the reels before show time.”

Max saluted Ray, then nodded and turned on the projector “Hey, can you bring me something to snack on?” Max asked. “I’m famished!

“Free meals are not in the contract, but in the spirit of professional courtesy, at least tonight, hang on, I’ll be right back,” Ray said with mild irritation before Max ran downstairs and plopped down in one of the plush new seats.

Ray went back into the lobby where his business partner Hal was behind the concession stand making popcorn. Hal, a grizzled fifty-five-year-old veteran of the film exhibition industry, asked Ray suddenly, “Did you ever throw up on someone while having sex?”

"No! That's disgusting! What am I, Charles Bukowski? Why even ask?"

"Just wondering if it's normal, that's all."

"Why, did you?"

"Maybe," Hal said with a shrug.

"Never mind this neurotic nonsense now. Can you bring Max a bag of that shit? He's watching the film now to make sure the fucking reels are in order, like that even matters."

"Shit? It's not shit. It's totally fresh! You watched me just make it! Even the butter is real!"

"Well, it won't be fresh anymore when we actually open, moron. Why are you making it now?"

"I'm hungry! I can always make more. And don't call me a moron."

"Can you please not eat all our god damn food before we actually sell any? You know concessions will be our main source of revenue. It's the only way we can compete with the god damn video cassette tape market."

"Like people can't order pizza while jerking off on their own couch. We need to get a beer license, I'm telling you, or else this whole project is doomed."

"Hal, why did you even go into this venture with me if you're going to have that negative attitude?"

"Just being realistic, Ray. And reality sucks. Look around. Single screen theaters like this are closing right and left. That's how we got *this* one, for a song, too."

"You didn't answer my question."

"I grew up in this business, Ray. It's in my blood. You were also basically raised in my dad's theaters, since your asshole parents were absent and movies were your babysitter, so it's in your blood, too. I told you we'd be better off with a repertory operation, with or without beer, but since you came up with most of the investment money, even if it was from selling hard drugs on the street, I went along. I'm just biding my time, though, till I'm proven right."

"Shit, Hal, even old movies are available in the home video market. Then there's cable TV. Next they'll let you watch anything you want on a personal computer. I admit, you're probably right. The odds are against us no matter what we show. I just don't know what the hell else to do with my life. Maybe I just should go ahead and die."

"Lighten up, already. Look, like I've been trying in vain to explain to you, classic movies are a communal experience, traditionally speaking. Porn doesn't need to be publicly exhibited to be appreciated. The less company the better, if you know what I mean. We'll try your way first, though, and if it doesn't work out, as it most likely won't, we'll adapt and experiment and grow over time, like any other independent business."

"Concessions provide most of the profits regardless of the type of movies we show, since those god damn rental and shipping fees suck up most of our budget anyway. And we can't get a beer license just like that, it's not easy. So, I beg you, don't recklessly consume all our inventory so we can have a fighting chance at least, please, huh?"

"We got plenty of everything food-wise, man. Popcorn, pretzels, hot dogs, candy, you name it. It'll be a veritable fuckfest feast. I'm more worried we won't have enough customers to justify it all. If we stocked beer as I've been strongly suggesting from the start, we could turn this place into a survivalist bunker if we had to, and with Reagan in charge now, we might. We're all gonna die soon, anyway. Meantime, just relax." Hal grabbed a handful of popcorn and threw it at Ray. They started giggling like little boys, reverting to their adolescent rapport.

"*You* relax, you swine-shit slurping, simian-semen-swilling *slob*," Ray said with mock disdain.

"Hey *fuck you,* you donkey dick sucking monkey-whore!"

"Kiss my ass, you facile fecal fetishist!"

"Bend over and I'll jam my manly fist up your torn, bloody butthole, you babbling baboon *bitch*!"

"You need to be hog-tied, horse-whipped and gang-raped doggy style by a maniacal mob of mutated maggots!"

"Yeah, while you wank on your little worm watching us, you pathetic puerile perverted *punk*!"

"Shut your pie hole and bring Max a bag of that crappy popcorn."

"Shut up."

"*You* shut up."

"Fuck you."

"Fuck *you.*"

"Am I interrupting anything, boys?" a silky voice said from the just inside the front door as lightning flashed and thunder boomed.

Ray and Hal turned to face the breathtakingly beautiful blonde wearing Ray-Ban sunglasses and a black leather trench coat. Her long legs led down to spikey, snakeskin pumps, and her copious cleavage practically popped out of its slick, sartorial confines, strongly suggesting she was nude beneath the coat. Her flawless complexion was like warm ivory.

"Who are you?" an entranced Hal asked at the same time an equally enthralled Ray said, "How can we help you?"

"Why, I'm here for the premiere of my film," the woman replied. "Don't you recognize me?"

She opened the trench coat, exposing her impossibly curvaceous and indeed completely naked body.

"Maybe if you took off the shades," Hal said with a laugh.

"Wait a minute, you're Alicia Armstrong!" Ray exclaimed. "You're the main love interest for the Cocktapus, right? Now I recognize you from the poster and press kit!"

"Holy shit!" Hal said. "I didn't know you were even invited! Why didn't you tell me, Ray!"

"I didn't invite her either!" Ray said. "Not that I wouldn't, I just didn't think any of the stars would come all the way to Seattle just for this."

"Well, frankly, I heard about the opening night in the paper, and since I'm from here, I thought I might as well show up," the luscious lady said. "This was my favorite theater growing up. In fact, I used to dance here when it was briefly a burlesque hall, back in the sixties."

"But you don't look a day over…" Ray stopped himself. Alicia Armstrong indeed only looked to be about twenty-five, meaning she'd been a professional exotic dancer at age five or so, by logical chronological calculations. "Anyway, whatever or whoever brought you here, very glad to have you!" Ray went up to shake her hand, even as her proximity overwhelmed his senses.

Alicia closed her coat and tied it shut before accepting Ray's gesture. "Thank you. And you are?"

"You can call me X-Ray," he said. "This here is Hal, my partner. Inside the theater is Max, our projectionist. He's checking on the print as we speak. Would you care to join the preview screening? We'd all be honored!"

"Sure," she said. "I haven't actually even seen it yet!"

"Neither have I!" Hal said. "Though we heard good things. It has quite a reputation. That's why we chose it for our premiere."

"Where did you say you heard about us again?" Ray asked her as they headed inside the cavernous auditorium. "We actually didn't spring for any ads yet, relying on word of mouth until we work out the kinks, so to speak. This is basically a trial run."

"Word gets around the underground grapevine," Alicia said. "I just thought I'd surprise you."

"You sure did!" Hal said.

"I guess the distributor told you?" Ray suggested.

"Perhaps," she said with cryptic caution.

But the graphic celluloid distraction looming before them quickly derailed the conversation. Up on the big screen, Alicia's voluptuous visage was sucking voraciously on one of Cocktopus's massive tentacles, while another tentacle pleasured her gushing pussy and yet another was indelicately probing her juicy anus.

The Cocktopus, at least in the "script," was a horrible and horny alien monster that had come here to mate with female humans, since all the women of his planet had been wiped out in a mysterious plague. Each of the monster's eight limbs was actually a penis that could ejaculate buckets of semen. On screen, Alicia's seven equally gorgeous "roommates" suddenly walked in on the sordid scene, and, impressed by both the power and number of orgasms being experienced and witnessed, immediately began disrobing, so the Cocktopus could fuck all of them at once. It was the most outrageously explicit and ambitiously choreographed sequence in the history of the genre, and all three men were pleasantly dumbstruck. No one moved for several minutes, hypnotized by the astonishing spectacle.

Finally sensing her compellingly charismatic presence behind him, Max suddenly turned around and immediately recognized Alicia. Since no one had bothered to formally introduce them, he shot up to greet her politely, then humbly sat back down, gaping at her lustfully in between glances back at her cinematic doppel-gang-banger.

"So, didn't the guy inside the rubber suit get to actually screw anyone?" Hal asked.

"What guy inside what suit?" she said, and they all laughed. Except for her.

"What is that sticky shit shooting out of him, anyway?" Ray said. "A mixture of milk and mayonnaise? Must've made you sick after a while, sucking and swallowing all that fake cum, not to mention wallowing in it."

"It wasn't fake," she said. "It was actually quite tasty. I couldn't get enough of it. None of us could. *Watch.*"

The males all adjusted the crotches of their pants as the bestial onscreen orgy intensified, with the "actresses" enjoying multiple orgasms as the Cocktopus showered them all with the icky liquid spraying from its eight limbs like uncontrolled fire hoses. The production values were indeed impressive for an allegedly low budget exploitation picture.

"The Japs are into this kinky shit," Hal said. "Plus, rubber monster suits are their specialty. I wonder if those creepy cocksuckers financed this sick little flick. They really get their jollies watchin' whores, excuse me, *women* gettin' raped by animals 'n' shit. Any idea who the backers were, Ms. Armstrong?"

"This movie was funded by outside interests," she said as she continued watching with unnerving solemnity, her sunglasses still mysteriously in place on her coldly beautiful face. "There's no need to be racist. Or misogynistic. Or homophobic, for that matter. Your kind can be so petty."

Suddenly Ray, Hal and Max grew very uncomfortable, shifting in their seats, and not just so they could adjust their leaking penises. Feeling morally ambushed by this feminist freak, they all remained silent for the remainder of the screening.

Once Max went up to the booth and brought the house lights up, Ray and Hal stood up and stretched. Alicia remained seated, still very quiet and eerily contemplative.

"Well, I'm gonna get ready to let the folks in, if there are any," Ray said with a nervous chuckle. "Would you like to come greet our guests with me? It would give them quite an unexpected thrill."

"There won't be any guests," Alicia said without moving her head, or even her lips, it seemed. "Only unexpected thrills."

"What…do you mean?" Hal asked.

She didn't respond, maintaining her mannequin-like stillness.

"I have a more positive prediction!" Ray said with forced optimism. "We're gonna sell out the house! Even without the benefit of advance advertising! That marquee alone will attract drive by traffic! We may even cause a few accidents, ha ha! Of course, that would've been easier if we could've promoted your appearance, but…"

Alicia smiled slyly and then slowly removed her Ray-Bans. Her glowing orbs had no pupils. She popped them out and discarded them like they were old mothballs. Next, she removed her blonde wig, followed by the synthetic skin on her phony skull-helmet. Then she stood straight up and took off the trench coat along with the rest of her fabricated flesh, finally revealing her true identity: Cocktopus itself.

The men all screamed and tried to escape out the fire exit as the monster's wildly flailing tentacles lashed out and grabbed each one by the throat, strangling them into submission. Since there were only three victims, the Cocktopus had five free arms with which to tear off their clothes and savagely ravage their orifices, filling them to the brim with its organic seminal fluid until they all literally choked on it. Additionally, the sizzling substance was lethally acidic, burning the flesh from their very bones, while disintegrating their internal organs, which flushed out of their anal cavities like gory diarrhea. But their intense agony stopped abruptly when the monster tore their limbs and torsos apart in a carnally carnivorous frenzy.

Several of the monster's voyeuristic companions—discreetly watching the entire gruesome scenario unfolded from the back of the theater—swarmed and devoured the remains of the men while one of the Cocktopi stood back and continued filming the festivities with an elaborate, portable alien camera.

A mile or so above The Rabbit Hole, a sleekly stylish spaceship hovered in the stormy skies, its occupants gleefully monitoring the mayhem via a massive console screen.

"*Cocktopussy 2: Movie Theater Massacre* will be our most successful porno snuff film yet," the eight-limbed director proudly proclaimed in its native tongue as the fully sated Cocktopi below left the theater just before a single blast from the spaceship set it ablaze, destroying any trace of what had transpired inside. "Especially in Japan."

"Damn!" said the corpulent, lonely man in a raincoat, staring forlornly at the raging inferno from across the street as fire engine sirens wailed in the distance. He had hoped to buy the first ticket. "Just my luck."

BEER RUN

Scott S. Phillips

Fortunately, the ringing of the phone snapped Radio Ketchum from the dream he was having, wherein the hot chick who'd just made herself available for his pleasure had suddenly turned into a large lizard. This transformation hadn't stopped Radio from partaking of the sweet business, however, and the entire thing had been more than a little unsettling. Combined with the vast puddle of drool beneath his cheek, he felt pretty okay with being awakened far earlier than he normally liked to get up.

Fumbling the cell phone from his bedside table — an old wooden crate standing on end — Radio squinted at the screen. His mom. He wished like crazy he had the know-how to set up a different ring for his mother, so he'd always know to expect unpleasantness, but science-y things like cell phone settings were far beyond his ability to comprehend. Tapping the screen, Radio lifted the phone to his drool-smeared face, where a strand of his stringy black hair clung in the spit-glue. "Hi mom — it's early."

"Not for people who work for a living," Radio's mom snapped.

For some reason, her words caused Radio to practically spring from the bed. He stood a lean and wiry five-foot-five, clad in nothing but an aging pair of tighty-whities, waistband separating from the britches in various places. A puckered scar adorned his lower left abdomen where a teenager had stabbed him while stealing a dime bag of weed Radio had recently acquired, fucking up Radio's favorite Van Halen t-shirt in the process.

"I have a job," Radio said. "I work at the bar for you, remember?"

"There's some wouldn't call that working, the way you do it," his mom said.

"I guess I don't quite understand why you're callin' me this early in the day when you could give me shit in person while I ain't workin' at the bar later on tonight," Radio said.

"I only do it out of desperation, I can promise you," Radio's mom said. "Justin Dangle flaked on me and I need you to manage Funboy for the day."

"Aw man," Radio whined. "Workin' Funboy is the worst — plus that girl's mean."

"Be that as it may, the task falls to you. And I need you over there right now — there's a truckload of liquor and beer on its way, and it's gotta hit the shelves fast, so get it in gear." With that, Radio's mom hung up.

"Shit," Radio said.

Radio's mom had bought Funboy Liquors less as a liquor store than as a way to avoid inconveniencing the meth-heads of Albuquerque's north valley, most of whom weren't willing or able to make the trek across town to Blue Corduroy, the bar where Radio normally worked (or didn't, depending on who you were speaking to). Funboy was pure shithole, crammed into a tiny free-standing building surrounded by even shittier buildings, perched on the edge of a truly godawful neighborhood. What with the meth-heads coming in looking to score, the once-a-week or so robberies, and the alcoholics stumbling through the place and occasionally vomiting everywhere, it was a living fucking nightmare to work the store.

And then there was Jayden Sykes. "What up, fucknut?" Jayden blarked as Radio entered the store.

"C'mon," Radio said, unable to muster up anything more.

Jayden was cute as hell but astonishingly hateful, wore black all the time and was tatted up like a Suicide Girl, which was fitting since she made Radio want to kill himself. He had once tried desperately to convince his mom to fire Jayden, but since the meth-heads were all scared of the girl, his mom wouldn't do it — figured Jayden's meanness ensured order would be maintained. Or at least what passed for order at Funboy Liquors.

Perched behind the cash register, Jayden cocked her head, whipping her jet-black hair out of her eyes long enough to glare balefully at Radio. "You're not the boss of me, I hope you know that."

"I'm just here for the day." Radio started to head behind the counter, then thought better of it. "How come Justin didn't show up or call in or anything?"

"What am I, his fuckin' mom? I don't know what that shithook gets up to in his free time."

"Jeez," Radio said, instantly regretting it.

"*Jeeeeeeeez*," Jayden imitated, enhancing the degree of whine in Radio's statement.

Embarrassed, Radio went to the front window and yanked the chain to turn on the neon *Open* sign.

"Do you *have* to do that?" Jayden asked.

"Yeah, pretty much," Radio said. "It's not like leaving it off will keep anyone out — I've tried."

A loud knock at the back door sent Radio skyward, eliciting a humiliating snort of laughter from Jayden. "Settle down, it's just Stevie with the liquor shipment."

Now even more embarrassed, Radio started for the back room. "It was just unexpected is all," almost adding another *jeez* before he caught himself. Making his way past the aisles lined with various snack food items, candy, and other convenience store staples (drunks do enjoy a can of potted meat every now and then), Radio pushed the swinging door open and went into the dimly-lit back room just as a louder thump sounded, like someone had thrown a sack of potatoes against the back door. Radio paused for a moment, then went the last few feet to the back door, where he slid the steel brace loose from its brackets and unlocked the three deadbolts.

Radio tugged the door open to find Stevie sprawled on the pavement, blood gushing from his nose, the truck carrying the liquor delivery backing out into the alley. "What the fuck —?" Radio took off running after the truck, glancing down at Stevie as he passed. "You're all right, right?"

"It was Justin Dangle and that Barry Bongos jagoff," Stevie shouted. "An inside job!"

Jesus fuck a shit souffle. As the truck roared off down the alley, Radio tugged his cell phone from his pocket and punched the speed dial for Funboy. Putting the phone to his ear, he skidded around the corner into the alley in time to see the truck turn onto a side street.

"Funboy," Jayden grumpily announced.

"Justin Dangle stole the goddamn liquor," Radio said, already breathing hard.

"Guess you'd better call your mom," Jayden said, unfazed.

"Or here's an idea — why don't you go fuck yourself." Radio hooked a sharp right, bounced off the wall of the building next door to Funboy, then raced along the narrow passage between the buildings. Out on the street, he saw the truck pass by, going right past Funboy. "You can see 'em right now, you look out front."

"Oh yeah, there they go," Jayden observed. "And *you* go fuck *your*self."

"You're gonna have to manage the store for a bit, I gotta get this liquor back," Radio said. "And whatever you do, *do not* say a goddamn word to my mom if she calls." Afraid of what sort of response he might get, Radio hurriedly ended the call and stuffed his phone back in his pocket.

Radio came out of the passageway like a spring-loaded snake popping out of a can of joke peanuts, making an odd leap, landing badly in the street and nearly tumbling. As he recovered, he shot a glance at the window of Funboy, disheartened to see Jayden pointing and laughing at him. The humiliation didn't slow him down, however, and he took off once again in pursuit of the liquor truck. There was no way he was gonna catch the thing on foot, but he figured if he could keep it in sight, maybe he'd be able to do —

Well shit — do *something*, although he had no idea what that might be, once it rolled to a stop.

He wasn't so sure he could keep running much longer, though. Radio hadn't gotten this much exercise since he was a kid and stole a bunch of candy from the Circle K, one of the clerks chasing his ass for blocks before finally giving up.

Radio guessed that was pretty much the meaning of that whole *ironic* thing, considering.

Fuckin' Barry Bongos. This had to be his idea, and he'd somehow convinced Justin Dangle to go in on it — and Bongos not out of the slam for a month yet. The crusty motherfucker had come to Radio's mom begging for a job, said a guy he knew in the joint told him she was always good to help out an ex-con with a little work. Mrs. Ketchum had put him on as a dishwasher, made things good with his parole officer, and this was how the bastard thanks her.

Up ahead, the truck slowed some. The passenger door swung wide and Justin came hurtling out, hitting the pavement and just sort of skidding along on his face for several yards. Some dude Radio didn't recognize poked his head out of the open door, smiled and waved, then yanked the door shut. Pouring it on, Radio hurried to where Justin lay in the street.

"Hey, asshole!" Radio shouted.

Justin sat up, dazed, his entire face a smear of blood and torn skin, gore running down his neck into his shirt. "Is my face bleeding?"

A little carried away in his haste, Radio couldn't stop in time and tripped over Justin, sending both of them sprawling. Justin screeched and started sobbing.

"He made me do it," Justin wailed, gingerly poking at his shredded face. "Ow ow! Fuck! I'm all fucked up!"

"You think you're fucked up now," Radio said, rubbing the tiny scrape on his chin where he'd hit the pavement, "just wait till my mom gets a hold of you."

"You can't tell her!" Justin shrieked.

At the end of the street, Radio saw the liquor truck move through a slow left turn, all the while Barry Bongos leering out the driver's side window at the two idiots laying in the road. "Why in hell would you and Barry steal the liquor shipment, anyway? You plannin' to sell it to your buddies or something?"

"I can't say," Justin said. "Barry would kill me."

"My mom's gonna kill you whether you spill or not."

"I told you, you can't tell her!" Justin shrieked once again.

"If you think there's any kinda scenario where this ends without me tellin' my mom you ripped her off, you're out of your goddamn mind," Radio said.

Frowning, Justin studied himself. The blood, having spread throughout the front of his shirt, was beginning to encroach upon his jeans. "I'll bleed to death before I give those guys up."

"Jesus," Radio said, getting to his feet. "Get with it, moron — they already gave *you* up when they tossed you outta the truck. Don't do 'em any favors."

"This was just a distraction to slow you down," Justin said. "I'll still get my cut."

Radio looked down at the bloody-but-confident mess. "You got about as much brains as a sack of used kitty litter."

"You just wait."

"Where's Barry live? Is that where they're takin' the truck?"

"Like I'd tell you," Justin said.

Radio walked over to Justin and kicked him in the nuts. Wheezing, Justin flopped over on his side, clutching his groin. "Let's give that one more shot, otherwise I'll give you another shot," Radio said.

Justin's strangulated voice was punctuated by sharp intakes of air. "I —" *hiss* — "ain't been —" *hiss* — "to Barry's place —" *hiss* — "'cause he's particular." He took a moment to suck in a few good breaths. "We always meet up at Frank's."

"Who's Frank?"

"Tooncen," Justin said. "Guy who shoved me outta the truck."

"Good friends you got. Where's Frank live?"

Justin glowered at Radio. "Ackerman Brothers Auto Salvage — he lives in the yard."

"What, in like a tent or something?"

"No, he's got a house kinda."

"Is that where they're headed?"

Justin hesitated. Radio drew back a foot, taking aim. Justin flapped his hands around. "Don't kick me again!"

"Then get to speakin'."

"I'm not sure if they're goin' there first or to the club," Justin said.

Radio kept his foot poised. "What club?"

"I don't know where it is — some sorta underground dance club, that's who we're selling the liquor to."

Sighing, Radio weighed his options. He sure as hell wasn't telling his mom about this — at least not yet. He could call Boone, see if he'd help out, but since he was all fired up about getting his private detective license or whatever, he'd want Radio to pay him for his time. "Where is this Ackerman Brothers?"

"Not far," Justin said. "Get out the Google Maps."

Radio kicked him in the balls again, stood over him as Justin wailed. "That's a bonus for fucking up my day in *sooo* many ways."

Not to give Justin any credit, but Google Maps knew its shit, leading Radio to the foreboding hellhole known as Ackerman Brothers Auto Salvage. In an attempt at stealth, Radio tucked himself behind a tree across the road from the place and scoped things out. Close as he could tell, the place had fallen out of *Mad Max Beyond Thunderdome* and landed in Albuquerque, suffering some pretty severe damage in the process. The fence around the yard was constructed haphazardly from sheets of tin, rolls of chain link, weather-beaten old boards and whatever else was handy. Junked cars were stacked three or four high throughout the yard, and a rickety trailer with a sign reading *Of i e* sat just inside the main gate.

Moving in closer, Radio peeked through a gap between a couple loose sheets of tin. Figuring the *S* in Brothers meant a minimum of two and maximum of who the fuck knew, he didn't want to take any chances. He jumped back out of sight (or as much as that was possible considering the sorry state of the fence) when two salty-looking dudes clad in filthy coveralls exited the trailer, both sporting caveman levels of facial hair. One of them paused, shifting his weight in the traditional cutting-the-cheese manner. Waving his hands wildly, the other one took off running. He who dealt it gave chase and the two disappeared down a row of stacked cars.

Peering around further, Radio finally decided there were only two Ackerman Brothers he'd have to contend with. Tugging carefully at one of the sheets of tin, he managed to slip through the fence with relative quiet. It wasn't until he was inside the yard that it occurred to him most junkyards have junkyard *dogs*, a thought that did nothing to make him feel more at ease. Hunkering low, he darted behind the nearest pile of shitmobiles and began making his way through the yard, listening carefully for any signs of slavering Rottweilers or Ackerman Brothers.

Now where in the hell would this Tooncen guy live in a filthy and disgusting junkyard? Surely not in the *Of i e*, right? Maybe another trailer parked somewhere. Radio ducked around a heap of old cars, coming to a dead stop as he found himself staring down a majestic heap of junk rising into the sky. A battered old school bus formed the base of the structure, with numerous other vehicles of all shapes and sizes sprawling out from it in three directions as well as straight up (using the word *straight* very loosely). It looked like some kind of Dr. Seuss fever dream, somehow remaining upright despite the precarious way the various cars and vans were welded together. Outside the door of the school bus was a small table and a couple beat-up plastic chairs. Here and there throughout the structure, makeshift curtains hung across the windows of some of the vehicles — no doubt rooms where a fellow would value his privacy.

Radio glanced around furtively, then crept towards the bizarre mountain of junk. Disappointingly, there was no sign of the Funboy truck, so maybe this wasn't Frank Tooncen's place after all. The school bus door was open, and with a last glance around to make certain no Ackermans or their potential dogs were approaching, Radio slipped inside.

The bus had been gutted of most of its seats, the few remaining having been rotated 90 degrees to look out through the side of the bus. A couple low tables sat in front of them. A breeze that might have been pleasant, if not for the stink of the salvage yard, drifted through the open windows. Radio figured this is what passed for a screened-in porch. At the far end, a hole had been cut through the roof, a ladder leading up through it, presumably to the upper floors. Radio cautiously approached the ladder and peered up through the hole, feeling an awful lot like any number of characters who had died horribly in any one of the *Alien* movies. "Hey, Frank?" he said softly. A moment passed. "Frank, you up there?"

Radio waited a good 30 seconds or so, then made his way up the ladder, poking his head up into the second floor, constructed from a hollowed-out van, the back doors removed to open into another roomy vehicle, although Radio couldn't tell what it was. This floor was decked out living-room style, with rugs scattered around, posters of scantily clad women taped to the walls, and a sagging couch off to one side. Across from the couch was a rickety set of shelves, a boom box perched front and center, numerous rap CDs piled next to it. In the unidentified vehicle was a card table with chairs around it, evidence of card games that had been accompanied by much smoking and drinking strewn across its surface and around the floor nearby. Another ladder rose up from that room, through yet another hole. Radio went to the table. Somebody's mail lay there, the envelopes torn open. Picking one up, Radio read the address: *Frank Tooncen, c/o Ackerman Brothers Salvage*. All right then. He dropped the envelope, noticing a Xeroxed flyer featuring some extremely shitty artwork lying near on the table. *DJ Rickie Rick's Private After Hours — Invitation Only*, with an address at the bottom. If it wasn't the underground club Justin mentioned, maybe there'd be someone there who could point Radio in the right direction. He grabbed the flyer, then went to the hole in the ceiling and asked if Frank was home. Again, there was no response. Radio listened real hard, hoping to catch some movement or breathing, but heard nothing. Eying the flyer once more, he decided he'd head on over and see what DJ Rickie Rick might be up to.

As Radio exited the school bus, he found himself staring at a rather large and heavily salivating dog. "Good puppy," Radio whispered.

Grrrrrrrr, the dog said.

"Shit," Radio said. He took a few deep breaths, then bolted.

The dog barked once, then took off after him.

"Shit shit shit," Radio repeated, seconds before the dog had his right calf in its mouth. Radio hit the ground hard, howling in pain, the dog snarling and shaking his leg around like a chew toy. Radio fired a kick into the dog's snout with his free leg, causing it to yip and let go. Hurriedly, Radio made it to his feet, limping on his dog-bit leg and kicking at the bastard what done it as he scrambled up a stack of junked cars. The dog jumped and snapped but its prey was beyond reach. Radio clambered to the top of the heap, pausing to check out the severity of his wound. His jeans were torn up and there was a lot of blood, but it didn't look too awful.

"Hey, motherfucker!"

Radio looked back to see an Ackerman Brother running his way, a very large wrench gripped in one mitt. Meanwhile, that damn dog kept leaping and barking and snarling below. The fence wasn't far off, but the only way he was gonna make it with that beast on the loose was to travel by car-pile, and that meant making some pretty spectacular leaps.

As he neared, the Ackerman whipped his wrench at Radio, narrowly missing his head.

Radio leapt.

And missed the next heap of cars, banging off its side and dropping into the dirt. "Son of a *bitch!*" he hollered, looking back to see the dog coming around one end of the pile he'd leapt from. Getting to his feet, he hightailed it towards the fence, the pain in his leg agonizing, the dog drawing ever closer. *And of* course, *the fucking fence doesn't have any gaps in it over here.* Springing upwards, Radio landed on the dented fender of an old Buick, then launched himself at the fence. He caught the top, scrambling up and over, dropping to the ground outside as he heard the dog bang into the fence on the other side.

Dog barking and an Ackerman hollering behind him, Radio split the scene.

Once again, Google Maps knew its shit, leading Radio through a long but accurately plotted walk to the address on the flyer he'd found. It was only when he was about halfway there that Radio realized he could've hopped in his damn car back at Funboy, when he first set out to pursue the liquor truck thieves, instead of hoofing it — and the throbbing, bleeding dog bite on his right leg made him even more unhappy that it hadn't occurred to him sooner. He'd paused shortly after escaping the salvage yard and sat down on a curb, where he took off his left shoe, removed his relatively clean sock (the right sock was too soaked with blood to be of much use) and tied that around his wound. Radio figured between dog slobber and whatever sinister forces might lurk within his old sock, he was gonna wind up with one hell of an infection, but at least the sock slowed the bleeding some. The pain was another matter, however, and by the time Radio arrived at the home of DJ Rickie Rick's Private After Hours he could barely walk, occasionally just hopping on his left foot to make forward progress.

Standing on his good leg in the street in front of the run-down house with the dirt yard, Radio sized things up. It was almost certainly the right place, seeing as how the Funboy truck was parked in the backyard. A cinder block wall surrounded the yard, but the wide gate at the top of the sloping driveway stood open, apparently not having been closed after Barry Bongos and his little pal Frank drove the truck on in.

Radio ducked — still on one leg — as Mr. Bongos himself appeared through the window at the front of the house, gesturing wildly and obviously yammering at someone. Realizing he wasn't actually ducking *behind* anything, Radio went right ahead and straightened again. Barry Bongos kept on moving, disappearing from view.

Well hell then. If they were in the house, there didn't seem to be anything stopping Radio from sneaking on into the back yard, hopping in the truck and driving it back to Funboy. For an instant, he thought about calling Jayden and letting her know of his good fortune, but figured she'd find some way to be mean about it. Besides, it'd make more of an impression if he just rolled up to the store and hopped out. Maybe she'd have a little more respect for him then.

Going into an awkward crouch, Radio limp-hopped his way to the open gate, where he ducked out of sight and took a peek into the backyard. The truck was parked with the ass-end out of sight behind the house. Holding his breath, Radio listened as hard as he could. After a moment, he decided there were no sounds of truck thieves and went on in, hopping as fast as he could towards the back of the house. Pausing there, he cautiously poked his head around the corner of the building. The truck's back door was open, as was the back door of the house, but there was no sign of anyone.

Radio hopped rapidly around the front of the truck and yanked the driver's door open. No keys. There went his swell plan. Standing on one leg, Radio contemplated his options. He could go on into the house, find Barry Bongos and Frank Tooncen and DJ Rickie Rick, appeal to their better natures, perhaps sweet-talk them into not stealing from his mean ol' mom, whereupon they would politely hand over the keys and allow him to be on his way with the truck.

Or he could simply flee, which was no doubt the smarter option, although it would mean calling his mom and telling her what had happened, and she would — as always — find some way to make it his fault.

The truck rocked a bit, shocks squeaking.

Radio stiffened. Somebody had climbed into the back and was shuffling around in there. The truck rocked again, and Barry Bongos backed into view, a case of Old Tree Frog whiskey cradled in his arms. The crusty ex-con was *literally* crusty, his skin dry and flaking in patches on his face, arms and hands, and even from places within his scruff of short black hair. This, combined with his prison-yard muscles and permanent scowl, made Mr. Bongos rather terrifying to gaze upon.

Radio's vision went into slow-motion as Barry started to walk towards the house, disappearing behind the truck. Amazingly, he hadn't spotted Radio, who released the breath he'd been holding.

And then Barry stepped back into view, a confused expression on his face, quickly replaced by one of rage. "Hey, fuckstick!"

Radio bolted in a one-legged tear around the front of the truck, only to find Frank Tooncen blocking his escape route. Dodging, Radio headed for the open back door of the house, realizing that entering the place was the stupidest thing he'd done all day, yet going right ahead and doing it. As he hopped through the messy kitchen, he glanced back to see Barry Bongos set down the case of whiskey, then run into Frank Tooncen as they performed two-thirds of a Three Stooges routine in an attempt to get through the back door.

Radio hopped out of the kitchen, down a short hallway, and into what would normally be the living room.

Welcome to DJ Rickie Rick's Private After Hours.

One wall had been torn out to open into what was probably an adjoining bedroom, but was now home to a raised dance floor. Soundproofing foam covered every inch of wall space and the ceiling, and the windows all had soundproofed shutters that could be closed when the club was active. Just to Radio's left was a DJ station with dual turntables and mixing board, and on the far-left wall was a small bar, where a chubby black fellow in shorts and a Hawaiian shirt — presumably DJ Rickie Rick himself — was stocking the shelves with stolen liquor.

And directly across the room was the front door. Radio kept on hopping, the puzzled DJ Rickie Rick watching him go.

Made it. Even on one leg, I actually made it. Radio grabbed the knob, turned —

To find the deadbolt locked.

That was all it took. Barry Bongos and Frank Tooncen were on him and the beating began in earnest.

"Don't do any damage to my club or get no blood on nothin'," DJ Rickie Rick said as a punch caught Radio in the ribs. "In fact, maybe go on and take him out back."

Seconds before a fist sank into his eye, Radio saw DJ Rickie Rick casually go back to stocking the shelves with his mom's liquor, then Barry and Frank dragged him out the back.

Radio made some meager effort to fight back, or at least cover his face, but Barry and Frank tuned him up for true, then left him lying in the dirt, staring up at the chassis of the stolen truck.

"Don't come back again, asshole." Barry punctuated this with an attempted kick to Radio's balls, catching him in the upper thigh instead.

The two criminals went back to unloading the truck. Radio remained there on his back long enough for each of them to make two trips back and forth, mostly so as to recover enough that he'd be able to hobble the hell out of there without catching another beating. When Barry and Frank went back into the house on their second trip, Radio slid out from beneath the truck, used the back tire to crawl to his feet — or foot, anyway — then hopped around to the rear of the truck. He gazed in at the stolen liquor for a few moments, then busted open a case of vodka, grabbed a bottle and went on his way, hopping with all the speed he could muster so as not to get caught with his twice-stolen bottle of hooch.

It was a long, slow, embarrassing limp-hop back to Funboy Liquors. Arriving at the store, Radio sat down on the curb out front and stared down the road in the direction he'd come.

After a few moments, Jayden came out of the store and stood behind him. "So, I guess that went about as well as I figured it would," she said. "Sure as hell looks like you got your ass handed to you."

Looking back over his shoulder, Radio grinned at the girl, then cracked open the bottle of vodka and took a long pull. Swallowing hard, he offered the bottle to Jayden.

"Ew, no way." Jayden shuddered. "Lips that touch swine will never touch mine."

"I don't even know what that means," Radio said, "except more for me."

"You're disgusting," Jayden said, then went back inside the store.

Radio took out his cell phone and jabbed the screen. As the phone rang, he took a longer swig of vodka.

"I sure hope you're not calling because you fucked something up," his mom said.

Not even a hello. "Mom," Radio said. "I quit." He hung up as she started to gripe at him. Turning off the ringer, Radio set his phone down on the curb, looked around at the shitty neighborhood he would never have to set foot in again, then took another drink.

God damn. It was good to be free.

The Aluminum Eagle

Axel Howerton

"Sorry pal."

The Woolworth's in the promenade is the last place on my list. I've been looking for this goddamn thing for a week. All over L.A. Every store in town. Every store out of town. Just today I've been to Jack's downtown, Kip's out on Fairfax, and hit Nalbands on Wilshire – and all the department stores, corner shops and pharmacy's in-between. Nobody had it. Not that I know what the hell I was looking for. The kid wants the spaceship from that space movie. His favorite movie. And, goddammit, he is going to get that stinking spaceship.

"You're sure? You don't maybe have one in the back? An *Aluminum Eagle*?"

"I don't even know what the hell that is, okay? Look, fella. I got a lot of people waiting here."

I tip my hat and maneuver back out of the crowd that's clamoring at the counter, shouting for toys and dolls and whatever else they can get their hands on last minute. Goddamn Christmas.

A couple of hippies, with their hands deep in jacket pockets, probably five-fingering themselves a Christmas miracle, stumble into me. One hand shoots inside my jacket pocket – pure instinct – to make sure the wallet is still there as I step out into the street. Santa Monica is nice, even in December. Mid-60's, warm enough that the kids zooming past me are in their shirt-sleeves, swirling and spinning on their little wheelie-boards, weaving around the old ladies with their shopping bags, the frustrated dads lugging boxes and bundles like shop-worn Sherpas. Some of the kids are hopping up onto the steps, leaping and sliding across the corners of fountains on their little maple-wood and polyurethane contraptions. Maybe the kid would want one of those things. A skateboard was a decent gift from old Pops, wasn't it?

I find an empty phone booth across the way, sitting idle and quiet. As much a bid at ten seconds silence as a real need to use the telephone. It's strewn with holly and lights, shaded under a propped up artificial pine that looks like it was made out of used pipe cleaners.

"Dad, don't worry about it. He'll love anything you get him. He'll just be happy you're here. You are still coming tonight, right?"

"Yeah, yeah. I'll be there sweetheart."

"Dad. Don't disappoint him again. He worships you. Just show up, okay? Spaceship or no spaceship. He's really looking forward to seeing you."

"Okay, I get the message."

Not that I don't want to see the kid. He means the world to me. I'm just not very good at Family – something my own kid is fond of reminding me – I was a shit father, and now I am on the road to proving myself a shit grandfather. There has to be something else the kid would love as much as a hunk of plastic.

A second dime clunks down into the innards of the machine and I crank out the number. Charlie picks up on the seventh ring.

"How deaf are you? Keep me waiting all day why don't you?"

"What can I do for you, Mighty Moe? You find that Aluminum Eagle yet?"

"Why the hell you think I'm calling your black ass on Christmas Eve, Charlie? No, I didn't find the goddamn thing. Your guys turn anything up?"

"You sure are some kind of detective, old man. How long you been searching for this thing? Two weeks now?"

"A month. Shut up about it already. I need other ideas."

"Moe, little man ain't that kind of kid. He ain't gonna give two shits about what present you bring him He just wants to see his granddaddy on Christmas."

"Ella seems to think I'm a disappointment to him." My shoulders tighten up at the weakness in my own voice. Anybody else, I'd never have uttered those words out loud. Charlie Moses was the only man on Earth I'd confide in that wouldn't have to pour a bucket of whiskey down my throat first.

"Moe, you a good man. You done right by Ella Louise. She may not see it all the time, but kids these days man… I ain't even heard from neither of my own in almost a year. You maybe weren't around all the time, but that's the job, baby. It's a new generation now. Mama's getting careers, Daddy's home on weekends, kids are out running wild in the damn streets. All of you take good care of little Mossy-Moe. He's a good kid, and you are a good grandfather, Moe Rossi. Now quit your belly-aching and just go grab that boy some tinker toys or some shit."

"Tinker toys? Are you kidding me, Charlie? Those were going out of style when Ella was little. You're no kind of help at all."

"You want some advice? Go fuck yourself. And get that boy an instrument. Maybe get him blowing harp, playing guitar. He's already playing the piano real good."

"What? And have him turn out like you, Charlie? Some itinerant musician, can't get paid, can't get laid?"

I chuckle at my own joke.

"I get laid, Moe Rossi. You just ask your Mama."

"*Ay*! *Stu cazzo*! No talking about Mamas, Charlie."

"Yeah, yeah. Merry Christmas, Moe."

"Thanks for nothing, Charlie."

"Ooh!" Charlie Moses shouts across the city and into my eardrum, "A trumpet! Get little man blowing horn! He'll be the next Satch..."

The click stops him dead before he can start into one of his tirades about the downward spiral of jazz in the twentieth century. I've only got so many minutes left in this life.

The box shudders around me and the receiver clangs against the metal of the frame, missing the hook entirely. I bounce against the plexiglas with a hard shoulder. I set the phone back proper, and spin in place, folding the door out of my way. Judging by the impact, I'm expecting some kid on a skateboard to be bleeding on the ground in front of me.

Somebody *is* lying prostrate on the walkway, but this kid is mid-twenties, dirty, disheveled, desperate. He's clad all in denim. Worn-out knees in his dungarees, dirt and sweat meeting somewhere in the middle layers of his equally worn jacket. He's clinging to a canvas rucksack – the kind you get at the Army surplus – and both the kid and the bag smell like they haven't been washed in years. He's got a scrub-brush beard and his hair is long in all the wrong places, like he doesn't keep it long, he just hasn't paid for a haircut in a while. He's weeping like a child as I drag him up to his feet.

"You alright, kid?"

He swipes a faded blue sleeve at his eyes and shrugs me off.

"Yes, sir. I'm sorry. Didn't mean to be a bother. Thank you, sir." He backs away, face flushed and eyes on the ground. It obviously wasn't the first fall he'd taken recently.

"Wait." I fumble for my money clip and finger out a five-spot. "Here."

The kid looks at me with water in his red eyes. His jaw sets, hard, and I can hear his teeth grinding from three feet away. His muscles tense and his eyes go to the wad of bills. One hand slips behind his back.

He breaths heavy and his eyes squeeze shut as he lifts his face up to the sky, the hand on the strap of his bag whitening at the knuckles.

"Thank you, but I'm okay, mister." He backs further away, stumbling through the bushes that line the promenade and back into the thoroughfare. I'm still holding out the bill when he turns and bolts through the crowd.

"Merry Christmas." The words tumble out of me broken, like a half-forgotten prayer. Goddamn Christmas.

Twenty more minutes of wandering provide exactly zero improvement of the situation. My meandering brings me down onto the boardwalk, blocks away, listening to gulls out on the beach screeching to be heard over the raucous noise of the people crowding the pier. More kids on skateboards, more dozy hippies and young girls in funky outfits, gliding around on roller skates. I guess nobody just uses the old flat feet anymore. Not even the beat cops. I watch, dumbfounded, as a couple of rookies roll their squad car down the promenade at a crawl. The one riding shotgun is leaning out the window, whistling at a teenage girl in a bikini with a sweater that's more hole than yarn. The cop is probably thirty-something, with sideburns down to his jawline and a moustache like Buffalo Bill Cody. In my day, you wouldn't see a single man below Commissioner with so much as a pencil-thin moustache.

Sinbad's looms up against the ocean, further down the pier. Big false front like a rusty stage set, promising me some small respite from the onset of the nineteen-eighties.

I push through from day into night, the interior of Sinbad's as dim and cozy as it ever was. Empty, cool and flickering with soft candlelight from every corner. My lungs twitch at the echoes of every time I sat in one of these deep, lush velvet chairs, the smell of cigar smoke and whiskey soaked into the carpet and the walls. A long, full breath takes me back and brings me a peace I'd never find out on the boardwalk, staring at the waves or sniffing the carnival odors of the boardwalk.

“Mister Rossi! *Buon Natale*!”

Navaho Joe, the bartender that never sleeps. His name is actually Navarro, or Navarres, something like that, but everybody calls him Navaho, despite the fact he’s obviously not anything close to Indian. He’s probably only a single generation removed from the old country. He speaks Calabrese better than I do.

“What brings you in tonight, sir?”

The smile creeps across my face all on its own. Respect. Old school regard, one man to another. Something I hadn’t seen all day – all goddamn week.

My legs cry out in joy as I ease onto the stool. I hear a groan come from somewhere in the middle of my back. “How you doing, Joe? *Tutt'a posto*?”

“Just fine, sir. Manhattan?”

“And a partridge in a pear tree, Joe.”

The overpowering stink of Aqua Velva and Brylcreem creeps across the room ten feet ahead of a booming baritone with a *New Yahk* clunk.

“Make that two, Injun Joe.”

Shit.

My shoulders slump under the weight, even before his giant mitts are on my shoulders.

“How the fuck you doing, Gentleman Geno?”

Jilly Rizzo. Colossal Man Friday to the self-declared Chairman himself. Jilly goddamn Rizzo. King of mumbled half-jokes and butchered nicknames. Already 0-2 and he’s only been in the room ten seconds.

"Nobody's called me that in thirty years, Jilly. Just *Moe* is fine."

"Alright then, *Just Moe*. How are ya?" Jilly Rizzo laughs harder at his own jokes than anybody else ever has, or probably ever will.

"I'm just fine, Jilly. Still kicking. Frank in town?"

Jilly twists his oversized frame into the stool next to mine, wraps a leathery old hand full of gnarled fingers with perfectly manicured nails around the drink that's already waiting for him. He squints through his tinted glasses like he's trying to read in the dark, then something connects. He shrugs it off and lifts the drink to his lips, pausing as my last question finally seems to reach his muddled brain.

"*Is Frank in town?* he says! You hear that, Injun? *Is Frank in town*? Of course, Frankie is in town. What the fuck would I be doing in California if Frank wasn't here? I'd rather be home in New York, with some goddamn snow, and a real goddamn Christmas. Y'know?"

"*Salute*!" I raise my glass to Joe. Hustle it down. Last thing I need is to get caught up with Jilly Rizzo and his boss. Christmas Eve in L.A.? Frank would be in some hotel nearby, holding court, ignoring his family, probably setting up a poker game with a bunch of washed-up used-to-be's. I was still looking for a spaceship for the kid.

"See you around, Jilly. Say hello to Francis for me."

One of those big mitts lands in front of me like a broken turnstile.

"Hey! Where you going so fast, Moe? Sit down, have a drink. For old times, huh? I don't know about you, but it sure don't feel like fucking Christmas out there to me. I could use some company."

Dumb as a stump, big as an ox, but he wasn't a bad guy. And I knew exactly what he meant.

"Come on. Sit down. Hey, Joey, set us up again." The other big leathery hand appears on the bar, huge diamond pinkie ring clanking against the oak, a crisp new hundred-dollar bill pinned underneath.

"Come on, Moe… One drink."

I always found it funny how Jilly Rizzo only managed to remember your name proper when his welcome was wearing thin. Something he learned from Francis – the lord and master of calming upset friends. Especially when he was the one doing the upsetting. Frank would needle and poke and abuse – all the way up to the point where you were ready to punch him square in that impish smirking face of his – and then he would reel it in, put an arm around your shoulders, slide you a nice gold watch, a stack of chips for the table, or the number of the svelte red headed cocktail waitress you had your eye on. Frankie Blue-Eyes, the man, the legend, the *mensch,* as Smokey Sam always called him.

I settle back into the groove of my seat before it's even had a chance to cool. An easy mark, I guess.

"Well, you already ordered the goddamned thing." I grumble, patting Jilly on his wide back. "Thanks Jilly."

"You and yours." He grins, shot gunning another full glass of Rye and vermouth.

Must go down like gasoline. I guess when you drink four or five bottles of Jack Daniels with the Chairman every night, a couple of Manhattans are like Shirley Temples.

"So, Frank's in town?" I ask with nothing else to say.

"You didn't hear about it? He just finished his next project, a whole opera-style *magnicum operatus.*"

"I think you mean *Magnum Opus*, Jilly"

"What'd I say?" All cow eyes behind his dark lenses. "Anyways. Frank's over at the Miramar. He sent me out to get some food. You know Frank. He's in L.A. He's gotta have La Barberas. *Jilly!* He says, *Pizza! La Barberas!* I just figured I'd stop in here and have a drink first. What the hell are you doing down here?"

"Looking for a present for my grandson. Some kind of spaceship thing from that space movie."

"The *Star Wars*? Yeah. All the kids are crazy for that bullshit."

"Something called an Aluminum Eagle? Aluminum Falcon?"

"*Millennium.*" Joe interjects from his corner, hands wiping deep inside a beer glass. "I believe it's a *Millennium Falcon*, Sir. My son and I saw that film four times. Very excited for the new one coming."

I stare at him for a second, feeling my age and ignorance. “Fuck sakes. No wonder everybody looks at me like I’m stupid.”

“Not going to find one of those tonight, I’m afraid, Mister Rossi. Biggest toy of the season, I hear.”

“Your lips to God’s ears, Joe. I've been all over L.A. And looking for this goddamn thing for two weeks now.”

Jilly Rizzo chuckles, possibly at some joke he heard last week that’s just now clearing the fog between his ears.

“What’s funny?”

“You. A Grandfather. Where the hell does the time go, Moe? I remember you fighting Johnny Ambrosia at the Gardens like it was yesterday. The Gentleman Geno, pride of Little Italy!”

“About a million yesterdays, Jilly. I’m an old man now. A goddamn stupid old man, can’t even remember the name of some hunk of plastic.”

“Fuggedaboutit.” It rolls out of his East coast mush-mouth like a benediction. “Hey. You want to play cards tonight? Frank would kill me if I didn't ask you.”

“It’s Christmas Eve, Jilly. I’m supposed to spend it with my family.”

“Without no present for your grandkid?”

“You make a good point.”

Like I said, I’m an easy mark.

The sun is fading away with the crowd as we stumble out into the boardwalk.

"Where you park down here, Moe? I'll give you a ride."

"Thanks, Jilly. I think I'll walk."

"Don't be stupid. Come on." Jilly Rizzo stumbles away up the boardwalk, big leathery mitt working the railing, both pulling him forward and holding him up. I follow him up, as much to make sure he doesn't roll back down as to get to the top and out on the boulevard.

Jilly's long white Cadillac is at the curb, a half dozen tickets jammed under the windshield. He swipes them away and stoops, half in-half out of the car, watching them twist on the wind.

"Fucking meter maids. It's goddamn Christmas Eve. They got no goddamn shame out here." He growls.

I lower myself into the passenger side and feel the bucket seat holding me close. It's more comfortable than my bed. At least it is until Jilly lets out a hellacious trumpeting fart. It smells like the dumpster behind a deli.

"Christ, Jilly!"

He gives with the blank look, no acting, he honestly doesn't know how he's offended. I let it go. I've been doing it myself lately. Like at the ballgame last spring. My son-in-law, he makes a big deal about it. Everybody around us holding noses and chuckling under their held breath. The kid, he just laughs out loud and hugs his old Pops.

"Look, Jilly. I really can't play tonight. Just drop me off at my car, alright?"

"Yeah, yeah. I get it. Just gotta make one stop first."

"Jilly…"

"Them barn burners Injun Joe was serving up… Doin' a number on my insides. There's a pharmacy right up the street."

"Come on in, Moe. Maybe they got something for the kid."

I lean back in my seat to look up at the faded blue paint and the thirty-year-old sign outside. Not exactly Woolworth's. What the hell? You never know.

There's a little bell rings when we walk in. The place is made up of two long aisles of the usual junk, with a medicine counter at the back. An impossibly ancient man in the short-sleeved white smock of his trade is barely visible back behind the desk, bobbing up and down on a stepstool as he reaches up to shelves of boxes and bottles of pills. They've got pills for everything these days.

Jilly doesn't even bother to look at the shelves around us. He's straight to the back, booming loud and important.

"Hey, old timer! You got some of them effervescence tablets? I got an ulcer like a sonofabitch."

I let them fade into the background while I eye the cotton balls, the enema kits, the vitamins… There's a little pile of plastic-windowed boxes full of Halloween costumes at half-price, garish plastic masks with the eyes cut out and a hole over the mouth. There's Frankenstein's monster and the Wolf-man, some kind of robot-thing.

I turn the corner and head back up the aisle, past lipsticks and band-aids, hair rinses, compression socks and canes, all the other accoutrements of getting old. As if Christmas Eve wasn't depressing enough all on its own. There's chintzy, ratty tinsel strewn round the tops of the shelves, which gives more the impression of a bomb having gone off than anything festive.

I finally come across one tiny section of wall with kids' toys, all in little plastic bags, hanging on hooks. Army men, whoopee cushions, cheap plastic ukuleles. There's a box at the bottom full of little stuffed toys. I recognize the characters from the cereal boxes I see the kid eating from on Saturday mornings when I pick him up for baseball practice. Fruity-something? Choco-whatzits? They've got cartoon monsters on them. He likes the Frankenstein monster and the blue ghost. I grab one of each. Better than nothing. Better than plastic guns or a goddamn skateboard, right? Maybe I should have got him an instrument. Who needs another cop like his old man, or an ex-cop like his old Pops? Let him do something beautiful with his life. Let him be talented and calm and beautiful. I look at the kid and I see everything I missed in his mother… everything I miss in my wife, rest her soul. He's so funny for a kid, you know? Really goddamn funny. And whip smart. Sharp as a fucking tack. I missed all that with his mom. I was hardly around for most of it, and by the time Betsy was gone, Ella was a teenager, practically a woman. Last thing she wanted was her old man around. Probably a miracle she didn't end up like one of those roller-skate girls out on the pier. I chalk that up to Betsy too. Now Moss, little Mossimo – named after his fuck-up old grandfather – he was going to end up with a stupid cereal box mascot and a gassy failure of a grandfather for Christmas.

The little bell dings again, thankfully forcing me to pull my head out of my miserable ass. I can't see the door from where I am. Probably some old woman who forgot to get her heart pills before the holiday, or one more old fart to liven the place up. I hear some kind of murmured ruckus from around the corner. Jilly's breathing hard enough for me to hear.

"Now, old timer! Give me the money! Hurry it up!"

I get the idea that I might want to play it safe, but man, have I had enough of this day. The last thing I'm going to abide by is some thug robbing an eighty-year-old pharmacist on Christmas Eve. I've got my .38 on my hip, and a sap in my pocket. I'm not as fast or as hard as I was twenty years ago, but I'm still no lightweight. The crack and groan in my lower back beg to differ as I creep low around the shelves and come up with a hitch in my hip. Just slow enough to lose the element of surprise.

"Drop it." I recognize the voice, the face. Scrub beard and hair all wrong. *Sorry. Didn't mean to be a bother, sir.* "Drop it!" The service revolver in his hand is steady and pressed right against the soft part of Jilly Rizzo's head.

My first thought is *acceptable losses*, but Frank would never let me hear the end of that, and who needs an enemy like him? I slowly crouch to one knee, put the .38 on the ground in front of me and raise my hands up, palms out. Then I realize I can't get up, and my hands drop by instinct to catch me before I wobble over onto one side or the other like a table with three legs.

"Hands where I can see them!"

I fold my other leg under and sit back on my heels, which hurts like a sonofabitch on my knees.

"Okay. Okay. Relax, kid."

He steps careful, keeping the business end of his pistol planted firmly in Jilly's temple, and kicks my piece away with the worn toe of his sneaker.

"Mind if I stand?"

"Don't move." I get a good look at the blueish tattoo smudged across his forearm as he swings the gun on me.

"Look, kid."

"*Don't call me kid, goddammit*!"

He's nervous. No, not nervous. Anxious. Desperate.

"What is your name then?"

He eyeballs me, focusing on the familiar old coot, instead of the stress of the situation.

"I know you." He blushes. Honest-to-God blushes. Not a bad kid, just in a bad place. Most of us have been there. I know I've been there once or twice. "I'm sorry, sir. Go ahead and get up."

I stand slowly, pushing myself up off of my knees and steadying myself on the counter on my way up. I'm playing it up a little, gaming my own weaknesses. Let him think I'm a step slower, a brick shorter, than I am.

"Now what's the problem here? What are you after?" I ask, hands up in the ol' peaceful *hold on* pose. "I don't think you want to hurt anyone; do you soldier?"

His eyes light up like Coleman lanterns in the dark. Wrong play.

"I am not a soldier! Not anymore. Get over there. Against the wall." He points my path with the barrel of his gun. Then he tosses Jilly Rizzo over to slump next to me.

"Aww. Why you wanna go pissing him off, Moe? Lay off."

"Come on, Jill. I thought you used to be a big tough." I say out the side of my mouth.

"Yeah, and now I'm an old man, and I don't want to get shot in the face. I ain't gonna die in California on fucking Christmas."

The kid is sweating Even more than Jilly. Anxious. Desperate.

"Nobody is going to get shot in the face. I just want the money, okay?" He swings the gun back around towards the counter. "Come on, old man! Hurry it up back there!"

The old timer behind the counter is knocking things over left and right, stumbling around like a drunk back there. There's a sputtering cough and a thud as he stumbles one last time and hits the floor.

"Jesus Christ!" Jilly hollers.

The kid turns to look over the counter before turning back and locking eyes with me. Now he's scared, unsure. He looks back again, calling to the pharmacist.

"Sir? Mister? Hey, you all right back there?"

He looks at me again, ready to panic. I need him calm and thinking straight.

"Maybe you should check on him." I offer. "We're not going anywhere. You've got all the guns, remember?"

He lifts the gun chest-high, the way they teach you in the service, then he sidles around the corner slow and easy, his obvious training taking over.

Once he's out of sight, Jilly is mumbling in my ear, "Whyn't you cold-cock him, Geno? You could take him."

"I'm still hoping he'll put one of us out of our misery."

There's a long moment of silence. Too long.

"Aww, shit! Come on! Breathe!"

Jilly stretches that turkey neck up and around, trying to get a peek.

"Whaddaya think is…"

I shush Jilly again and chance a peek around the counter myself. The old pharmacist is lying on the floor like a discarded fish, and soldier boy is alternately pumping at his chest and pinching his nose shut then leaning in for what they call the "breath of life". He's trying to save him.

"*Goddammit! Come on*!" Pump-pump-pump. Breathe-listen-breathe.

I'm not sure how much the frail old man can take, soldier boy is sure to break some ribs at least. His gun is lying out on the floor, three or four feet away. My own training takes over. I'm calculating who gets there faster, who gets hands on pistol first. I'm playing scenarios in my head – angles I can jump at; punches I can throw – not too many of them come up Moe Rossi.

He jumps when he feels my hand on his shoulder.

"Hey. Let me call an ambulance. You go out the back. Let me take over."

He slumps back against the counter, face down into his own hands and weeps.

I pick up the gun and pocket it.

Then I reach for the phone.

"Aww shit. Goddamn it all. Stupid. Stupid." He's pulling at his hair, frustrated, angry, desperate.

"I'm never gonna get Amy home. Loser. You stupid fucking loser!"

The old man gasps a breath beneath me and groans.

"Hey." I shake the kid by one outstretched leg. "Hey!"

He looks up with rivers of mud tracking his face. The tears cutting streams through misfortune.

"He's gonna be alright. Look, he's breathing. He'll be alright."

A ragged breath hitches in the kid's chest, some small relief breaking off a chunk of the dark cloud over him, dropping it into the sea. I know that feeling.

"What the fuck is goin' on back there?" Jilly shouts. I can picture him, still sitting there like a lump with his hands up in the air, waiting to get shot right between the lenses of his oversized shades.

"Shut up, Jill." I holler back.

"Didja get 'im, Moe?"

"Shut the fuck up, Jilly."

The soldier boy takes a deep breath and composes himself. The old timer practically snoring beside us.

"Thank you." The kid says, red faced again.

"What's this all about, son?" I ask him. "You seem like a decent sort. You need money? Is it drugs? I know some of you fellas came back from Vietnam with a hook in you…"

"I'm just trying to do right by my wife, our baby. She's due any day now and we're stuck out here. We are so far from home, sir. I'm just…" He wells up again, strikes his fists against his temples. Tough guy stuff. They teach you that too. No emotion, no weakness. Just training. Follow your orders, do your job. Never mind what happens when you're back in the world and there's no Sergeants or Captains to direct your every move.

"Where you from, kid?"

"Joe. My name is Joe, sir."

"I'm Moe, Moe Rossi." I hold a hand out and he takes it. "Where you from, Joe?"

"I'm from Hoboken, sir. But we live in Bethlehem now… New Jersey."

I laugh. I don't mean to, and it puts a queer look on his face to hear it, but I can't help myself.

"Joe from Bethlehem, trying to get his pregnant wife home on Christmas. I'll be a son of a bitch."

He finally gets the joke, and the two of us are guffawing like a couple of goofballs behind the counter, the old man sawing logs like he was home in bed, instead of laid out on the linoleum of his third-rate drugstore.

"What the hell is going on back there? Can I get up? This floor is killing my lumbago!" Jilly bellows from the other side of the wall. That makes us both laugh even harder.

"What the hell are you laughing at?" Jilly grumbles, finally brave enough to poke his bald head around the corner of the counter.

In the ten minutes we're waiting for the ambulance, Joe tells us his tale. A job offer that turned out to be a scam, another scam that turned out to be a flat-out robbery. A procession of dead-ends and broken promises leading to Joe getting desperate enough to commit robbery to get the money for train tickets home to Jersey. There's a dozen stories like that for every single block of sidewalk in Los Angeles. But Joe's also got a wife, seven and a half months pregnant, waiting in a sleazy motel on the outskirts of Palmdale. Probably wondering if the last crack of the savage club of fate is the one that leaves her alone and destitute with a baby born in a dirty bathtub on Route 138, halfway between the lights of L.A. and the deserts of Death Valley.

The sirens wail in the distance. Time's up. I take Jilly to one side and explain the situation.

"Jilly, what do you think Frank is going to say, if he finds out you met a kid named Joseph, with a pregnant wife on goddamn Christmas Eve, and you didn't do everything you could to help them? A hometown kid from Hoboken, and a G.I. to boot?"

"Yeah, I guess he wouldn't like it none too much. But what do you want me to do about it?"

I fight the urge to slap his head like Frank undoubtedly would do.

"Frank sent you out for pizza? Keep the ten bucks you need for that, give the kid the rest of your roll. Frank never lets you get out of bed without enough money to bribe the Queen of England for him. How much do you have on you? Two, three grand?"

"Most of five. Minus the drinks and the pepto."

I give in and tap him a light one behind the ear.

"So, give the kid the money and let's get him out the back door. In fact, you drive him out to pick up his wife, I'll get Frank his pizza."

"Then what do I do with them?"

"Take them to the airport, you mook!" Jilly gives me a confused wall-eyed tilt of the head. "We're not making a seven-month pregnant woman take the train all the way to Jersey."

"But Frank won't…"

"If you go now, you'll be back in plenty of time for the card game, Jilly. Unless you'd rather stay here and talk to the medics, and explain the whole thing to the cops?"

I needed Jilly to take the kid, mostly because I couldn't trust Jilly Rizzo to talk to the police that would be on the way as soon as the old man started talking to the paramedics.

The light bulb over his head took a minute to fire up, but there was the unmistakable glow of electricity beginning to flow between his ears.

"I promise, I'll get Frank his pie, alright?"

"La Barberas. Pepperoni and sausage. Large."

"Yeah, I got it Jill. Same fucking thing he eats every night he's in town. Would you get out of here?"

I shake the kids' hand, wish him a safe trip, and I watch him climb into Jilly's land shark. As they pull away from the curb, he cracks the window in a hurry, craning his head back towards me. I think he's got something else to say. Then he waves his hand in front of his face. Jilly Rizzo strikes again.

The old man is sitting up, asking questions. I tell him he must have slipped, maybe had a heart attack, but a nice kid, a good soldier, saved him. He grumbles under his breath, asks me to lock up when the medics take him away. No cops, no more trouble. I lock the front door and turn out the lights. I snag a little bottle of J&B off the shelf and toast sundown. I call my daughter, make my feeble apologies. I take the Frankenstein monster and the little blue ghost, and I leave a twenty on the counter. I lock the alleyway door behind me and drop the keys in the mail slot.

La Barberas is closed. Goddamn Christmas Eve.

Frank doesn't care about the pizza once I tell him the story. He laughs his ass off at me when I tell him about the Aluminum Eagle, like he's any younger or any hipper to these things than me.

The game goes on most of the night. Sammy's there, singing Christmas carols at the piano. Jilly comes home around midnight to report on his Christmas miracle, which Frank brags about as if he had flown them on his own back. Jack Daniels and Chivas and champagne flow 'til dawn.

I pull up at my place as the sun is cresting the east side of the city, Ethel Bradley, my landlady, nurse, confidant and occasional paramour scurries out of her apartment with a sprig of mistletoe in one hand, and a big brown parcel under her arm.

"Sweet baby Jesus, Moe!" She groans, as I move in for a quick peck on the cheek. "You smell like the inside of Dean Martin's soiled asshole!"

Always a charmer, but she makes up for it with her bedside manner.

"Not too far off, sweetheart. What's this?"

"Somebody from 20th Century dropped it off about an hour ago. You must have some kind of friends, having things delivered on Christmas morning!"

"Thanks Ethel. Merry Christmas."

I take the box into my place and drop it on the table. I start the coffee and strip down to my skivvies, stare at myself in the bathroom mirror and curse myself for a lousy, broken-down old screw-up of a grandfather one more time, before I have a second look at the box. It's addressed to me alright. 20th Century Fox logo on the label, special delivery from F.A.S. – *Francis Alberta Sinatra.* But the card inside is in Jilly's unmistakable chicken scratch.

Didn't think Frank would mind.

Called in a favor.

Kid says "Thanks"

– Jilly

Navaho Joe was right. It is a goddamn *Millennium* Falcon.

Liner Notes

The photographer dangled from a rusted rung as two floors worth of fire escape ladder dropped into the alley, smashing against a dumpster with an echoing *bang*. *Fuck, fuck, fuck.* Someone must have heard, probably called the cops. He braced for the wail of sirens, and grabbed the next rung, feeling it crumble under his palm. *Fuck.*

Stop. Breathe. You're overreacting again.

Nobody was calling the cops in this part of town. Not over a scruffy guy hanging off a busted ass fire escape in the dark. How the hell was he going to get back down?

Just think about the money.

He pressed on, distributing his weight as the skeletal structure creaked and popped, until he reached the seventh floor. Once there, he hooked his leg through a sturdy-ish rung and caught his breath, scanning the apartment windows across the alley. Most blazed with light, but not hers. She'd be home soon, though he wasn't sure of the time. He'd pawned his watch and cell phone just to keep afloat this month. The only thing separating him from the hobo mumbling down in the alley was his beloved camera. He extracted it from his rucksack, slipped the strap around his neck, and waited.

You'd think he'd be the patient sort, given his job was to stake out folks committing insurance fraud, but not tonight. He'd been fired. Due to quote 'conduct unbecoming a professional' whatever the fuck that meant. Yes, some choice shots had made it onto Tumblr, but he'd blurred out the faces. Who'd have thought his boss would recognize his daughter's ass tattoo. Creepy old fuck. But whatever. A lot of people saw those pictures and one even sent him a message offering him cash for more. Serious money. Just go to this address tonight at 11 p.m., get some shots, and rake it in. Revenge porn, blackmail, or a personal collection. Not his business. Soon he'd be rolling in dough, enough to maybe go legit and start that publishing company he'd dreamed of.

The apartment light went on and he raised his camera. The heavy telephoto made his perch awkward, but worth it for the paycheque. A woman in a black sundress stood at her kitchen counter, pouring herself a drink. Had to be her. Hot curves and a crazy head of curls. He watched her down half a tall gin and tonic. Stretch. She walked across the room, pulling her dress over her head as she went.

Right. Here we go.

He snapped shots until she almost slid out of sight behind the edge of the window. *No! Move back.* Just a goddamn half-foot. The edge of her hip poked out, revealing a flash of scarlet panty. He slid as far as he could to the edge of the ladder rung. She turned around and bent over, round ass coming up. Jesus she was hot. He leaned further out, straining as the ladder groaned. Or was that him? With just his knee and one foot holding him, he held the camera at arm's length and watched as she started to pull down her panties. Money shot.

You're gonna be fucking rich.

Crack.

The ladder broke, taking him down into the darkness.

He opened his eyes. Blinked. Lights from the apartments above threw fractured shadows into the dumpster where the cardboard must have broken his fall. Talk about luck. He was officially rich. Once he pried himself out of here and staggered home.

Except his legs wouldn't move. Or his arms. Or anything.

A face peered over the top of the dumpster. The hobo. He glanced side to side, then climbed in, crawling over in a greasy cloud of old sweat and cigarettes. Waved a hand in front of the photographer's face.

Help! His plea came out a faint gurgle.

With a broken tooth grin, the hobo picked up the camera.

Snapped a close up.

"I'm gonna be rich."

Traditional noir is a well-respected and well-represented genre, but not everyone can be Joel Cairo or a Lou Ford or Walter Neff. No, there's a good chance that criminal type lurking in the alley is no mastermind.

Sometimes it's two brothers in a Buick Skylark – no license plate and stuffed full of gas cans – looking to drive a straight shot from Nova Scotia to Mexico, and instead of an epic road trip they panic at the Maine border and nearly get shot for suspected terrorism. A crime story so dumb it has to be real. That's what we wanted for this book. We asked for boneheads making disastrous decisions in their pursuit of the perfect crime, and damn did these authors deliver. Whether they're clueless, incompetent, or just plain unlucky, you'll laugh and cringe and wonder if maybe, just maybe, it actually happened. Because some of this stuff, you just can't make up.

Sarah and Rob, your Knucklehead Editors.

About the Authors

Jason Pearce (Two Kangaroos Chained to a Piss Pot) is an Ontario-based fiction writer who is originally from rural Newfoundland. His work has appeared in the literary magazine *Grain*, as well as anthologies in Ontario and Newfoundland. He has written several novels and is still deciding which one to refine for possible publication.

Craig Faustus Buck (Honeymoon Sweet) has won numerous awards for his neo-noir novel, *Go Down Hard* and his short stories, most of which are available free at **www.CraigFaustusBuck.com**. He is also a screenwriter, having written and/or produced network series, pilots, movies, and miniseries for more years than he cares to admit. Some highlights include the seminal miniseries *V: The Final Battle*, the Oscar-nominated short film, *Overnight Sensation* (starring Louise Fletcher and Robert Loggia), and the famous episode where *The*

Incredible Hulk drops acid. But most importantly, he is a pitmaster extraordinaire.

Laurie Zottmann (Work At Home Opportunity! Perfect for Single Moms) is a mental health writer, hot mess single mom, and a grown woman who sometimes can't get out of bed to fix her own snacks. Her articles and essays can be found in regional parenting magazines across North America, in two smashing anthologies from *Coffin Hop Press,* and on her blog, **www.DarkLittleCritter.com**, where her imaginary raccoon helps her sniff out the strength in depression, anxiety, and ADHD.

Michael Bracken (Sex Toys), recipient of the Edward D. Hoch Memorial Golden Derringer Award for lifetime achievement, is the author of several books and more than 1,300 short stories published in *Alfred Hitchcock's Mystery Magazine*, *Black Cat Mystery Magazine*, *Ellery Queen's Mystery Magazine*, *Espionage Magazine*, *Mike Shayne Mystery Magazine*, *The Best American Mystery Stories*, and many other anthologies and periodicals. He lives, writes, and purchases sex toys in Texas.

Most of **Pamela Kenney's (All in a Day's Work)** writing, from books and short stories to non-fiction articles and essays, contains an element of humour. Whether writing about a jewel thief (and the cop who loves her) in the *Diamond* series of books or a humorous essay for the Globe and Mail, Pamela likes to keep it light. But it's in her *Buttercup* books, where "all heck breaks loose" and the quirky residents of a fictional small town get free rein, catching bank robbers and finding treasure maps (and that's just the seniors in town). When Pamela Kenney isn't writing; she can be found on stage, doing improv. Information about Pamela Kenney's books can be found on her website: **www.PamelaKenney.com**

Billionaire, superhero, philanthropist - **Chris R. Young (Thick as Thieves)** wants to be all of these things and more. But alas he finds it easier to dream about it instead of actually doing it, so he's a writer, and not even a very good one. Join him on his haphazard journey through his own head as he encounters idiot villains, talking animal detectives, quirky multi-dimensional office staff, time travelling thugs bent on plagiarism, and stories that may or may not mean something.

Tom Barlow (Hic) is an Ohio Writer whose works straddle the literary, crime and science fiction markets. Over 80 stories of his may be found in anthologies including *Best American Mystery Stories 2013*, *Best of Ohio Short Stories #2*, and *Best New Writing 2011*, and many periodicals including *Hobart*, *Temenos*, *Redivider*, *The Intergalactic Medicine Show, Crossed Genres*, *Mystery Weekly*, *Red Room*, and *Switchblade*. He is also author of the noir crime story collection *Odds of Survival*. More information may be found at his web site, **www.tjbarlow.com**.

Jaclyn Adomeit (Scratch and Sniff) is an MFA candidate in creative writing at UBC. She is a writer and cartoonist whose short stories have appeared in magazines and anthologies in Canada, the US, and the UK.

Brent Nichols (Go Fish) is a suave playboy with an indefinable air of mystery and a regrettable penchant for self-aggrandizement. He likes good beer, bad puns, high adventure and low comedy. He's never been seen in the same room as Batman, but that's probably just a coincidence. He has two novels with *Bundoran Press*, and self-publishes military science fiction under the pen name Jake Elwood.

Steve Passey (Johnny Money) is originally from Southern Alberta. He is the author of the short-story collection *Forty-Five Minutes of Unstoppable Rock* (Tortoise Books, 2017) and chapbook *The Coachella Madrigals* (Luminous Press, 2017). He is part of the Editorial Collective at *The Black Dog Review*.

Steve Brewer (Cemetery Plot) has published 31 books over the past 25 years. His first novel, 1994's *Lonely Street*, was made into an independent film starring Jay Mohr, Joe Mantegna and Robert Patrick in 2009. *Bank Job* currently is in development in Hollywood. A former journalist, Steve teaches in the Honors College at the University of New

Mexico. He and his family recently opened a bookstore, Organic Books, in Albuquerque's historic Nob Hill district.

Will "The Thrill" Viharo (Soft Opening) is a gonzo pulp fiction author, lounge lizard, dog walker, cat daddy, and B movie impresario. For many years he was host, programmer and producer of the live "cult movie cabaret" (B movies, live bands and burlesque) "Thrillville." He now lives in Seattle, WA with his wife, actress/educator Monica "Tiki Goddess" Cortes, and their two cool cats, Tiki and Googie. His "psychotronic noir/existential pulp" novels and novellas include *A Mermaid Drowns in the Midnight Lounge*, *Chumpy Walnut*, *Freaks That Carry Your Luggage Up to the Room*, *Things I Do When I'm Awake*, *Down a Dark Alley*, and *Lavender Blonde*; the Vic Valentine, Private Eye series starting with *Love Stories Are Too Violent For Me*; and two sci-fi epics with *Scott Fulks*, *The Space Needler's Intergalactic Bar Guide* and *It Came from Hangar 18*. His short stories have been published in several anthologies and collections. He writes a movie column for *Bachelor Pad Magazine*, and he is the founder of Thrillville Press. Swing by Will's cyberpad "Thrillville" for literary cocktails anytime at **www.thrillville.net**. Cheers.

Scott S. Phillips (Beer Run) has written all kinds of stuff: films, TV, books, comics and even dialogue for talking dolls. He's the author of *Gun Up* (featuring Boone Butters, who Radio Ketchum considered phoning), *Man With*

Chihuahua, and the *Pete, Drinker of Blood* series, as well as several other books. Scott wrote the screenplay for the cult action flick *Drive* (Dacascos, not Gosling), and twelve episodes of the CW Network's *Kamen Rider Dragon Knight*. Perhaps most importantly, he once performed as stand-in for the legendary Lemmy in the video for Motorhead's "Sacrifice."

Axel Howerton (The Aluminum Falcon) is the punch-drunk author of the Arthur Ellis Award nominated detective caper *Hot Sinatra*; the zombie novella *Living Dead at Zigfreid & Roy*; and the noir hitman fable *Con Morte*. His next book, *Demon Days* continues the urban fantasy-meets-noir “Wolf and Devil” saga that began with his modern gothic fairytale *Furr*. His short work has appeared in dozens of publications the world over, though not so much as to draw attention. When he’s not smashing genres like a rampaging hulk, Axel can be found building books like this as an editor for Coffin Hop Press, polishing his fleet of mostly unremarkable guitars, or frequently teaching small children to pummel each other with gloves on.
Visit Axel online at **www.axelhow.com** or seek him out on social media as **#AxelHow**

Robert Bose (Senior Editor) has a fondness for bumbling criminals, absolute darkness, and Bourbon, though not necessarily in that order or at the same time. He's the editor of numerous books and anthologies for Coffin Hop Press (including *It's a Weird Winter Wonderland* and *Baby, It's Cold Outside*) and the author of myriad short stories including the fiendish collection, *Fishing with the Devil.* When not writing, editing, and running unfathomable distances, he spends his time annoying his wife, pestering his three troublesome children, and working at becoming a madman.

Sarah L. Johnson (Co-editor) is an ultramarathoner, curly hair gladiator, and indie bookstore events wrangler. Her short fiction has appeared in *Shock Totem*, *Room Magazine*, *Year's Best Hardcore Horror Vol. 2* (Comet Press), and the Bram Stoker Award nominated *Dark Visions 1* (Grey Matter Press). She's the author of *Suicide Stitch: Eleven Tales* (EMP Publishing) and *Infractus* (Coffin Hop Press). She is also co-editor on two previous Coffin Hop Press anthologies: *Baby It's Cold Outside* and *The Dame Was Trouble.*

COFFIN HOP PRESS

NEW CRIME. NEW WEIRD. NEW PULP.

Visit us online at
www.coffinhop.com

CPSIA information can be obtained
at www.ICGtesting.com
Printed in the USA
LVHW091921031019
633137LV00001B/3/P

9 781988 987194